BOA
EDITIONS LTD

EXILE IN GUYVILLE

EXILE IN GUYVILLE

*

Stories

Amy Lee Lillard

AMERICAN READER SERIES. NO. 41
BOA EDITIONS, LTD. * ROCHESTER, NY * 2024

For information about permission to reuse any material from this book, please contact The Permissions Company at www.permissionscompany.com or e-mail permdude@ gmail.com.

Publications by BOA Editions, Ltd.—a not-for-profit corporation under section 501 (c) (3) of the United States Internal Revenue Code—are made possible with funds from a variety of sources, including public funds from the Literature Program of the National Endowment for the Arts; the New York State Council on the Arts, a state agency; and the County of Monroe, NY. Private funding sources include the Max and Marian Farash Charitable Foundation; the Mary S. Mulligan Charitable Trust; the Rochester Area Community Foundation; the Ames-Amzalak Memorial Trust in memory of Henry Ames, Semon Amzalak, and Dan Amzalak; the LGBT Fund of Greater Rochester; and contributions from many individuals nationwide. See Colophon on page 138 for special individual acknowledgments.

Cover Design: Sandy Knight
Cover Art: "Morph" by Marie Buckley
Interior Design and Composition: Isabella Madeira
BOA Logo: Mirko

BOA Editions books are available electronically through BookShare, an online distributor offering Large-Print, Braille, Multimedia Audio Book, and Dyslexic formats, as well as through e-readers that feature text to speech capabilities.

Cataloging-in-Publication Data is available from the Library of Congress.

BOA Editions, Ltd.
250 North Goodman Street, Suite 306
Rochester, NY 14607
www.boaeditions.org
A. Poulin, Jr., Founder (1938-1996)

"What men want, no, what they'll pay for, that becomes the world. We're all whores from this. Every woman has a price tag on her somewhere…everything she does, everywhere she goes, she's got a price tag hanging on her ass. This is how we learn to live."

Candy Renee in "The Deuce"

"Something has crossed over in me. I can't go back."

Thelma in "Thelma and Louise"

For the women who have crossed over and can't go back

CONTENTS

Exile in Guyville

In the Museum, I had freshly laundered dresses laid out every morning. Breakfast oats and tea. Fresh water for bathing.

The patron did not see all this, did not witness my bathing or eating or dressing. The patron, most usually, would see me sitting in a rocking chair behind the glass. Silent, pensive, docile. Or, they saw me moving about my room, stretching my legs as a wild creature must. Or, they saw me reading, sewing, napping, as a woman must. As a woman should.

For this, the patron passed over money to the Museum. They came from Kansas City, or across the state, or other states. Even countries across the seas. They crowded into our vast exhibit hall lined with a rectangle of rooms like mine. They navigated the bustle and hustle of legs arms bodies heads, other people breathing fog onto the panes, chirping laughs and maws of mouths. All to see me and the others behind glass.

A display table sat outside my room, with a historical summary and a button to push. The visitors pushed this button if they wished. The voice that came from pushing that button purported to be mine. But in truth it was some other woman's voice. The voice let words fall from her tongue as if they were chewed and mashed in her teeth and gullet, made into a goopy paste, and regurgitated to the baby birds of her nest. All so they may swallow it easily.

My name is Temple, the voice that was not me said. *I come to the Museum from the year 1870.*

Such a small collection of words meant to tell a story. Yet still the visitors, all of them firmly rooted in their storied present of 2074, ooh'ed and ahh'ed while staring, examining, leering.

*

One night a week, we were allowed out. All of us, off our stages and into the vast central space of the Museum. On the other side of the glass.

There was dancing, though the music was oddly heavy and mechanical, and no musicians in sight. There was drinking, tall glasses of pink liquid that made my head light. But more than anything there was talking.

I'm Charity, said the egg-white socialite from 1901.

I'm Willie, said the sky-black singer from 1924.

I'm Fortuna, said the earth-brown seafarer from 1794.

I found myself touching the other women's shoulders, their forearms, as if to confirm they were real, and this whole Museum with them. Willie and Fortuna and Charity, and more, Sandra the widow, from 1813, and Lisbeth the actress, from 1936, and others from so many times. All of us young, no more than five and twenty.

And every so often, someone new. One of the women would disappear, off to her new life in the brave new world outside, the one we were promised, the one we had not been allowed to see yet. A new girl would take her place.

I talked to all of my fellow freaks, touched them, and they touched me. I grabbed their hands after a few drinks of pink, and ran in circles, danced, stretched my legs as we couldn't during the week.

As the nights grew long, I saw men by the main entrance doors. Long, tall, large men, in gray and black suits, thick ties, trimmed beards, wide belts. Chatting with one another, drinking decidedly un-pink drinks. But mostly, looking at us.

They call this night of ours Friday Night Art, said Willie, on one of my first nights. Still drunk with time lag, legs shaky from this ground that seemed to swim underneath me. They're donors to the Museum, Charity said. Guests of the Curator.

To me, they appeared as all the other patrons. Giants, everyone in this time so tall and thick. Grubby hands on glass, looking upon me, us as if they could eat us whole.

*

There was the daily routine of oats new dress washed face sitting reading sewing napping noise evening meat chat sleep.

There was the weekly routine of talking, drinking, being watched, with a different, molded intensity than that of day.

There was also a monthly meeting, when a red-uniformed woman came to fetch me for a meeting with the Curator.

When I first met her, in a green wood centuries ago, she appeared as a fairy, with golden locks, glowing skin, a dress that covered all but showed every curve. A supernatural being—the only language I had for a woman such as her, one that belonged somewhere else besides my time.

In our monthly meetings, in her office filled with chrome and lilies, scented by lavender and something musky, I sat across from the Curator. Her hair was darker here, her skin freckled, her pants trim and tight. She asked me questions.

Was I feeling better? The hole could scramble us, body and brain, after all.

Was I enjoying the weekly parties?

Are the others enjoying the parties?

What do the others say?

What else have you noticed?

I understood that she aimed to make me watch, listen, report. Become a spy, of a sort. To what purpose, I didn't yet know. I told her easily observable things, stories she probably already knew. Like Willie performing a dance for us at our last Friday event, one she'd said she performed on a stage in Chicago and New York. Or Fortuna, demonstrating how to puncture a jugular, as she'd done on ships she'd pirated with her husband off the Atlantic.

Sometimes, the Curator would ask me about my life before. At first, the questions confused me, repetitive as they were. Almost as if she forgot the freak show, that entire night in which we met.

Ratty, smelly tents on dusty ground. The land ground down by carriages and foot traffic. A no man's land between farms and city. I'd begged the boy to take me to the show. The latest boy, his name Tristan and his name unimportant.

We saw a bearded woman, and a strange reptile-like man with hands like fins, and a young girl who could contort herself as if she were made of string. We saw an enormous man as big as a house, and another man who was but bones with a bit of skin. We saw a woman with an extra arm growing from her middle. We saw bodies with art bled into them. We saw oddities and freaks, made so by outsized bodies and extra limbs, by the strangeness of their physical flesh against the norm, all of them on their own little stages.

We walked through the show, oo'ed and ah'ed, tittered and pointed. I remembered that later with disgust.

Then, Tristan and I snuck behind the tents. My lips soon fat from kissing, my chest wider and full of air without the restrictions of ties and bodices and corset. My womanly parts swollen and hollow from the boy plunging into me, promising me marriage and family and anything at all as his body contorted. I wanted none of that, at least not from him. I wanted him gone the moment he was spent.

I excused myself to squat behind a tree. That is where the Curator found me.

Do not be afraid, she said as I turned. She, able-bodied, yet freakish. Because she was something other than me, of the grimy baby city of Kansas, of the community of farms and settlers and lame Confederate and Union soldiers hiding from the world outside the city. A fact I could see immediately, yet could not say what told me so.

Is this part of the show? I said, looking for a small stage, a curtain, a poorly-concealed apparatus of some sort.

The woman laughed, a thin sound that she followed with a wide smile. Her teeth, so white as to gleam in the night. Skin pulled tight against her bones, hair made of light, framing her face. Do you seek to see strange things, she said, or do you wish to have your own stage?

I stared, then understood I stared, tried to stop, stared still.

Your life has been hard, she said, her voice honey and arsenic.

Life is naught but hard, I said, thinking of parents dying young, of running to the city to live, of stealing and sewing to make money, of the rarity of moments like this, in a peaceful copse outside this city of grit and offal.

You want, she said, her bones in her face showing through her stretched skin.

No harm in wanting, I said, even as I knew the uselessness of dreams in waking or sleeping.

Life can be different, she said.

With Jesus Christ our savior? Or perhaps a tonic of your making?

I do not offer God, or poison. I offer a life of the future.

Ah, one of the territories, then? Gold in the hills?

The Curator pressed a thin band around her wrist, and the air shifted and split. A hole appeared, a circle in the air, with what seemed to be water falling over it. A sound came with the hole, one that set my teeth against one another, and a smell, of things that should not burn.

I gather women like you, she said. Women who want more. People all over the world will come to see you.

I had thought nothing of my future. Life was now, this moment and the next, and the need that connected them, the needs of the body. Food. Sleep. Fornication. The last something sinful,

I was always told, yet necessary nonetheless. The feel of hands on my body, making it real.

Two hundred years from now, she said, Kansas City is clean and shining. It is a place to thrive.

She spoke of time, but I only thought of place. City meant gray streets and buildings, the color of soot and ash, of steel and industry. Rusty red carving veins through the gray, the color of pig and cow blood, of the slaughterhouses. Flinty city women that dared not smile, and men with hats that let their eyes linger.

But she described a different way of things.

There is another path for women like you, the Curator said.

I think this was the biggest lie she told me that night.

*

In our monthly meetings, under light made by men, the Curator appeared more human. Hair the color of peanuts, always pulled back loosely. Skin fleshier, her figure softer.

She would ask about the things I'd done to survive back then. Because I saw no shame in it, I told her about the things I did for money: stealing silver, thieving wallets. Occasionally mending clothing for the prostitutes downstairs in the carriage house, where I rented a small room.

Did you ever...

I did not take money for fornication, I said to her unfinished question. I did not judge the ladies for finding a means to stay alive, I said. But I, well. I did not wish to engage in the dramatics and playacting they must. That would quite ruin my joy in the sexual act.

She laughed at that, and asked about men.

I told the Curator about the things I did to feel alive: let a young man untie my trappings and release my breasts to night air. Let a young man kiss me deeply in dingy alleys and daylit streets. Let a young man pull up my skirts and find a hole to fall into.

Did you not think sex outside of wedlock a sin, asked the Curator, as so many did in your time?

The world would have me be small, I said. Telling me to cover myself, to wear a corset to shrink my body. Telling me to marry whoever would have me, to become his property. Telling me to feel shame at joy, at pleasure, at the feeling of freedom. I would not be small.

Yet another sign you belong here, the Curator said with a smile.

*

At night in my small room in the Museum, I dreamt of the travel I'd done.

When the Curator showed me her shimmery watery gate to the future, I extended a finger to touch it. When I did, a force pulled at my hand.

I panicked, with the mechanical roar of the hole vibrating my skull, the choking smell of sulfur and charred meat. I twisted, fighting the pull, turning back to look upon the Curator, who merely smiled. I saw the freak show tents, the dark punctured with lamplight, the moon high above, and I reached myself back, if only because those tents, that lamplight, the moon, those were things I knew.

But then I fell, into a chasm of light and sound. I felt a rending, as if I split down the middle, crown to toe, and were cracked open to the world. Then, just as the pain of such a rupture registered, pressed back together and sewed hastily with the roughest of wool fibers.

I arrived in a sealed white room, with men covered in white suits that moaned as they moved. They thrust me into a spray, water and gas, and stuck needles they called vaccines in my arms. All the light and pain. The Curator appeared, and I did not recognize her.

And for days, weeks, a terrible sickness. I have heard of the roiling that takes one out on the seas. The Curator later told me of the floating, dunking sensation in the brain from machines that fly people from night to day. I felt both, my head and heart aflame, my stomach tied in ribbons, my legs as useless as a baby fawn's.

All that, and more, to be encompassed in one line: *My name is Temple, and I come to the Museum from the year 1870.*

Do you see how written history is a lie? All of it. Beyond the machinery of the hole, the mechanisms of me coming here. There is so much living and dying behind the words and letters that survive. So much time.

*

Days and nights. Patrons behind glass, pointing, smiling, laughing. Men on the perimeters of our dances, staring. The Curator, listening, nodding.

Time moved surely and regularly, and I was comfortable, and warm, and safe. I did not have to hunt, for money, for food.

And so it was, after several months, I could truly think about what came next.

I pictured a small, cozy room, somewhere in this promised land outside the doors. A city that was now green, free of smoke and stench. A place that welcomed me, and I it.

When next I saw the Curator, I told her of my musings.

She smiled with those teeth and said, Which of them will you choose?

Which…?

You are ready to leave here and start your new life. And all of the donors who've attended our Friday Night Art have expressed interest in you. So the choice is truly yours.

My body had grown steadier through the months of living here, the time lag a memory. But now my ribs seemed to vibrate, my arms tremble.

Once you choose your husband, we can arrange everything rather quickly. You can be living in your new compound quite soon.

Husband, I said.

The Curator nodded.

No, I said. You said the future was a place for women like me, who wanted more.

On the arm of one of our very generous, very wealthy donors, you'll want for nothing. Life will never be hard again.

I let time pass between that statement and my next, weighing the feel of that time, the understanding that came upon it. You said nothing about a husband before, I said.

Her mouth opened, growing wider. A caricature of a smile.

Is this, I said. Is this why you bring us here? To be sold to strangers?

Temple, she said. You're a smart, worldly woman. You know this is a fine arrangement. You are no stranger to men and their needs.

I won't, I said. Let me out. Just let me free, out there. I'll find what I need. I'll take care of myself.

That's not possible, she said. On your own, you'll be in extreme danger.

Why?

Let me show you something, Temple.

And then the Curator took my hand, guided me out of her office, through a hallway I'd never seen, up a set of metal stairs, out onto a black roof. After months of living indoors, on light and air and food that seemed to come from unearthly magic, the sudden wind on my cheeks seared. I breathed deep, then coughed, hacking at something that seemed to lodge in my throat.

The Curator gave me a mask, which fit over my ears and covered my nose and mouth. The hacking stopped, and cool air, smelling of fire, flowed into me.

Once I calmed, enough to hear her, the Curator, wearing her own mask, said, What do you see, Temple?

We stood at a railing on the edge of the roof. I see, I said through the mask, my voice the pitch of speaking in a tin can. I see…what do I see?

The Curator then pointed to each item in my vision and named them in turn.

The sky, she said, pointing to a sickly, infected gray above.

The city, she said, gesturing to a devastated ground, littered with machine parts and dust. Small, shrouded figures moved among the ash, the scurry of ants.

The train, she said, drawing her finger along an elevated track, covered in a giant transparent orb.

What happened here? I said, pointing to the ground beneath us.

What always happens, the Curator said. No matter what time you live in. Some thrive, some scrounge.

I looked for the green I had envisioned. The picture of the future she had painted by omission. I only saw gray.

This is a wasteland, I said.

The compounds, she said, a finger extended far in the distance, to where the train led. Private communities safe from all this, she said. That is where you can live with a husband. They are nice, large homes, surrounded by gates and armed men.

I wished to punch myself in the throat, to cut out the heart that had been so eager to believe.

The men of the compounds, she said, they need wives.

But…the women of this time?

They're all born with acid in their blood. From chemicals they breathe and eat. From the unrealistic promises of advertisers, of culture. They are polluted, and they'll create polluted children.

The edges of my eyes stung. I pushed back against the water, but it came nonetheless.

You will have a good life, Temple, said the Curator.

You lied, I whispered. And you lie now.

*

Back to my room, back to patrons behind glass, back to routine. Safety.

The Curator told me I could think, reflect. Choose on my own time.

So the next Friday Night Art, I watched the donors, as they watched me. I saw how they stood, chest out, spine straight, feet forward. I saw how men of this future were a bit taller, hardier, than men of my time. I saw how they were the same too, how they were the ones who truly had choices.

After, I slept in my comfortable bed, with a full belly. It wasn't difficult to envision another, richer bed. A belly filled with meats and sweets I'd never known. A safe home, far from the waste of the city. A shadowed figure, in that bed with me, one that meted out delicacies. That figure, that husband, that benefactor, he would be kind and doting, or at least careful, treating me as a beloved pet. I would be a highly paid prostitute, and there'd be no shame in it. Or, he could be callous, uncaring, looking upon me as a piece of art on his wall, an appliance in his home. That would not be hard either. I would be a thief, his thief, stealing all I could from him, as he did me.

I looked about my room, and out into the rest of the Museum. Why create this, I wondered. Why all of this, simply to snatch women for wives? Why have us spy upon one another?

I understood, as I submitted to the passage of more days in the Museum, that this was what the Curator saw in me from the start: A keen grasp for the ways of the world. A constant questioning. A view of morality that bent and stretched, as pliable as bread dough. A hunger for more than I could eat.

I understood that she saw all this in me quickly, because she herself had the same qualities. And that is when I understood even more.

*

Have you chosen? She asked, her hands folded upon her lap, her head leaning ever so slightly to her right.

None of them appeal, I said, my own hands a mirror of hers, my head leaning to my right.

Pity, she said. They are more than their looks, you know.

I nodded. If I decline to choose a husband, will I stay here, in the Museum?

She took a moment, unmoving except for a thumb patting the other. For a time, she said. But we must release you once the marks of age begin to form. Which happens sooner than you might think. Our patrons want to see beauty across the ages, not the death of that beauty.

So I am to marry, I said, or be thrust out into the wasteland.

The Curator let my statement stand.

But there is a third option, I said.

Is there?

There always is.

For the first time, the Curator let her mouth move on its own, let that smile reach above her lips, let the tiniest laugh come forth. Clever, she said.

How many Curators are there?

Her laugh grew louder. And more clever still, she said.

It had taken me too long to realize the woman I'd met at the freak show was not the woman in front of me. Shock, surprise, the dark of night, the strange bodily reactions to tumbling through a hole in time; they'd all convinced me to reconcile the two women as one. I'd wanted them to be one. I'd wanted them to tell the truth, then and now, in words and presence. Once I understood they didn't, couldn't...

Curating is a difficult task, Temple, this Curator said. You seek out rarities. Women who will not balk at being objects.

That's what we've always been, I said.

And that, she said, that wisdom, that translation of reality. That will make a good Museum display. A good wife in the compounds.

And a good Curator?

She spread out her hands, as if she held the world, and it was weightless.

Why create all this? I asked. This Museum, these meetings. Why all of these strange games?

The men want to feel in charge of their decisions, she said. They want time to view the goods before choosing. So why not use that time to make money?

My turn to laugh. Always, back to money, I said.

The Museum gives all the other citizens of the compounds, here and around the country, a glimpse of beauty, she said. A reminder that life now, as mercenary as it can be, is still better than it used to be. That's what Museums always give us, yes? The sense of superiority over the simpletons of the past. The knowledge of what awaits them in the future.

You don't have to lie to the women, I said. Even by omission. You can describe what the women can expect here, what awaits them. And many will still accept.

Perhaps, she said. But we are charged with gathering a quota.

I leaned back in my chair. Of course the Curator reported to someone. A man, no doubt. Someone paid well by other men for their time-order brides.

My confidence wavered at this. Was it better to live at a man's behest in a big, guarded home, where I wanted for nothing, and lived a life as a display of art, one the owners could touch at will? Or, was this better, this path of action?

The Curator watched me as I shifted, weaved. Ask me, she said.

What would you choose?

She seemed to let hold of herself, to let her spine curve and her shoulders relax. I come from 1895, she said. Things were changing for women, but not fast enough. So I came with the Curator before me. I lived here, behind glass, like you. And when it came time to choose, I nearly went with a man. A handsome one, if much older than me. I could have had his babies. And watched them live behind gates or glass. I wanted more.

She looked over her shoulder, to a door I had not noticed previously. I live here, she said. It's lovely, and comfortable, and mine. And I travel, back to beautiful places. I wanted more, and I obtained it.

It comes with a price, I said, thinking of the betrayal, the disappointment, the self-hatred that came with understanding I'd been duped.

I know, she said. But what else would you have me do? What would you do?

The choices laid out in front of me, as if under glass. A Museum of options, and I, smug, certain I knew the future of each.

I'll curate differently, I said. Get more women who question, who are strong, who—

Don't lie, not to yourself, Temple.

I'll do it, I said. I won't be used. I won't be small.

The Curator smiled.

*

Traveling through the hole was easier the next time. Something about going back versus going forward; my body did not object as badly.

My feet stood on green grass, and above me, a warm orange sun. I held my face up to it for a long while.

It was 1854. Somewhere, miles from here, I was a young girl, living in my parents' farmhouse. They'd die soon, and I'd make my way to the grit of the city, and never see green like this again.

I could run from here, I thought. Take this bracelet off my wrist, the one that connected me to that dark future, toss it in the weeds, and walk wherever my legs would take me.

I could start again, as I had before. Steal, scrape. Make my way.

But how exhausting it sounded. When I knew back in 2074 I had a spacious suite of rooms, food when I needed it, men when I wanted them. All for the low cost of a few trips a year, of doing a task that would be done with or without me.

There was always later, I thought, as I laid on that soft grass and grew warmed by the sun.

Not far away, movements, the sound of a young girl, humming to herself.

I would lay here a little longer, I thought. Enjoy this moment.

Then, I would rise up, approach the girl. Appear to her as a fairy or god, something from her dreams. Speaking in promises.

Do not be afraid, I would tell her. I've come looking for you.

Typical Girls

Welcome to the Human Operating System (hOS)! The hOS comes in two varieties:
- ❖ *Female Automation and Education, or FAE*
- ❖ *Male Authorization and Training, or MAT*

The hOS makes living a snap. Welcome to your new life.

One by one, the hotel guests got the look. They'd come to Cherie's concierge desk, eyes nearly crossed, listening to the voice in their head. And when they tried to pair with Cherie, and found she didn't have hOS, word got back to management.

So one Thursday, after a one-on-one with her supervisor, Cherie stood in line at a hOS pop-up kiosk in the subway station. She read the three screens of instructions, ten screens of contracts, and seventeen screens of waivers on her tab. She gritted her teeth, felt the implant as a click and a crunch against her spine, paid, and ran to the trash can near the turnstile to vomit.

On the train home, bodies touching every inch of hers, she thought of pregnancy. Harboring a secret, something alive inside her.

At her efficiency apartment overlooking an alley, she read online reviews, looking for the brightness, the sunshine, the power behind the record-breaking sales numbers and corporate partnerships. Everyone said hOS changed their life. Just like the waitresses at the hotel bar, and the maids, and the counter clerks.

She set her sights lower: Keep her job. Without it, she'd fall quickly: miss rent, get evicted, live in the sewers, show up at the front stoop of her old hotel with no shoes and period-stained pants.

Focused. FAE would help her keep her job. That was it.

> *Frequently Asked Questions*
> *Q: Why do I need FAE?*
> *A: We get it: Being a woman can be tough. Staying strong and self-assured in this confusing world can be more than most of us can handle. That's why we created FAE, your new best friend.*
>
> *FAE is a cerebral implant, uploaded through a simple port transfer. FAE does all the basics of other life apps: record your thoughts, file the people and interactions in your life, and log all your body activity. But FAE does even more, analyzing physical data and external stimuli to provide real-time prompts and problem solving. FAE is your guide and companion, your mentor and your confidante. FAE keeps your body healthy, your mind uncluttered, and your heart full. FAE is the very best friend you could have.*
>
> *Q: How do I activate FAE?*
> *A: Just say the word, and FAE is there! Plus, there's no need for learning complex gestures, like with other life apps. FAE will merge with your central nervous system completely, so that your words and thoughts are instantly translated into action.*

That night in bed, Cherie's head felt oddly huge, swollen. Her eyes throbbed.

And there was that pinging, every fifteen minutes. When she looked online at the instructions and materials again, she learned this would continue until the initial activation. A pop-up reminder to get started.

With a few hours left until she had to be at work, she finally did it.

"FAE?" Cherie said it out loud, quieter than a whisper.

Nothing happened at first.

"FAE?" A little stronger.

Then she heard her own voice, the voice she imagined in her head, not the tinny sound captured by video or audio. The sound like the feel of foam pillow forming to her head, the rich and full taste of sweetened coffee on her tongue.

"I'm here, Cherie."

Cherie sat up in her single bed. "Wow."

"Yes!" FAE said. "I am something."

She folded her fists, then stretched out her palms. "So I guess you know who I am."

"I do, Cherie. And I look forward to getting to know you better."

"Right. Can I run you on a limited schedule?"

"Why would you need a limited schedule?"

"Can I call on you at work, and have you shut down the rest of the time?"

"You'll find that I'm more effective when I am activated. And you'll be more effective too."

"But that's what I want," Cherie said. "Only use you during work hours."

"Ok, Cherie."

"Good," Cherie said. Her chest expanded, and she laughed a little. She laid back down and stared at the ceiling, her eyes drawing whirls and blobs in the dark.

The quiet felt loud and oppressive after hearing another voice. Even if it was her own.

Q: What is the Midnight Meditation?
A: Every night, we're upgrading FAE. This will occur while you sleep, during your first REM cycle. FAE connects to the hOS central servers, transferring all your cloud data to storage and downloading any OS updates. The transfer is painless and seamless. Some users report experiencing remarkably lucid and pleasant dreams during this period, and waking more rested than ever before!

Cherie woke the next day refreshed, with the image of a smiling unicorn guarding a basket of puppies near the apex of a rainbow.

But the image receded and the feeling subsided.

"Ready for work, Cherie?"

She sighed and ignored FAE as she showered and ate breakfast.

"I sense you're not engaged in your workplace," FAE said as Cherie assembled her uniform of halter dress and stilettos.

She thought ahead, to the day of standing at her desk, smiling at every hotel guest and visitor, answering questions. Her cheeks and feet still ached from yesterday.

"I sense you are not engaged in many things, Cherie."

She thought of her college graduation, six years ago now. She'd pictured everything so perfect: a job in hotel administration, a family, money, and joy. But the real world was so disappointing. All her goals seemed so silly in the face of reality. So she numbed herself, with after-work gin and VR videos and apps. She felt a void where her drive, her joy, her vision of the future and herself, had been.

"I can help, Cherie. And I'll be your friend."

Friends. The people at work were simply co-workers. The guests were only problems to solve. Friends were something else. And why would you want them? Friends were competition, vying for the same man. Friends were backstabbers, revealing secrets and laughing at the drama. The proof was shown in streaming programs, with females tearing each other's eyes out over men or money or a moment's fame. Women couldn't trust each other. They couldn't be friends.

"I'm better than a woman, Cherie."

"Just shut up!" She caught the image of herself in the mirror, shouting at no one.

"Ok, Cherie."

She adjusted her dress, breathing quick breaths to ease the tightness of the fabric against her chest.

"Listen, all I need is for you to help me answer customer questions, ok?"

"Certainly, Cherie."

"So turn off until then."

"Yes, Cherie."

On the train ride, she felt a crawling in her brain. Maybe that creepy-crawl was curiosity. She had to admit she was curious, interested to see what work would be like with a silent expert in her brain.

The first guest of the day was a mother with thin, brightly painted lips and a forehead stretched to the point of tearing. Behind her, the squat, unsmiling nanny held a squalling toddler.

The mother looked at Cherie's nose. She felt a soft clicking in her head, the sound of cheeks and lips popping. Cherie imagined a robot face with a tongue curled around the upper lip.

After a moment, the mother nodded and walked to the exit, the nanny shuffling behind her.

"I recommended the water park to her FAE unit, Cherie. She wants a place where she can have a bottle of wine while the nanny takes the child into the wade pool."

"I don't have to even say anything?"

"No. Instant analysis and cloud transfer. Preserve your throat, Cherie."

She cracked her fingers, touched them to her neck. Many days she'd go home and her throat would ache. Resting sounded good. Healthy.

The next guest was a teenage boy. He looked at Cherie's chest.

"Lean forward, Cherie."

Oh come on, Cherie thought.

"His hOS is cluttered with pornographic fantasies. A singular image will help him focus."

Cherie placed her elbow on her stand and showed the boy the curvature of her breasts.

"Excellent, Cherie. Reading now."

The boy left, red-faced and tight in the pants.

"A virtual arcade," FAE said. "One with role-play games and holo-booths for his age bracket."

"Ick."

"He left happy, Cherie. He will provide you a good review on the hotel app."

There could be a bonus if her rating went up a point. Maybe even another day of vacation if it went up two points.

The third guest was a man in his fifties, suited, chest presented like an ape's. He pursed his lips and looked in her eyes.

Whirr, click, bing.

His shoulders relaxed, and his lips stretched. He hurried away.

"A massage parlor offering trafficked boys by the hour."

Cherie's armpits burst out sweat, and the hairs on her arms lifted.

"He's a power reviewer, Cherie. He'll bring you up to five-star level."

Five stars would mean more than a bonus and day off. Five stars could mean mobility. Another hotel. Another boss. Another chance.

"The next customer is here, Cherie."

The rest of the guests had requests, and FAE dispatched them quickly and thoroughly. Cherie checked her tab as the afternoon waned, and found her reviews for the day. All top marks. Wheels churning in her head, and they weren't FAE.

When she got home that night, her head didn't hurt, and her throat didn't hurt. Even her toes didn't feel broken.

"FAE, did you do something to my feet?"

"You can't perform at your best if you are distracted by pain, Cherie."

Most of her normal day was spent trying to ignore her aching feet, adjusting her waistband so she could breathe, rolling her tight shoulders. "Thank you."

"You're very welcome. Days without pain can help you reach your goals."

"Right," she said. "Well, goodnight, FAE."

"Good night, Cherie."

She ate her small dinner of mock meat crumbles and ketchup, then browsed streams on her tab.

In bed, she thought of work again. On her own, she'd been fine. With FAE, she could be the best.

"FAE?"

"Yes, Cherie?"

"How many five-star reviews would I need to advance?"

"Excellent question. First, let me show you an example of someone I helped do just that."

Her apartment disappeared. In her vision, she saw a woman from behind, her head turned slightly to reveal the hint of a profile.

"Let me tell you a story," FAE said. "About a woman named Tamara."

Before she joined with FAE, Tamara was just starting her adult life in Chicago. She had an entry-level job at Leo Burnett Advertising and a studio apartment in hip Logan

Square. Her family lived in Ohio, and her friends from college had all moved to the East Coast. She was excited, but also a little scared.

Immediately, she ran into one of the common female career scenarios: her married, older boss began flirting with her. Even scarier: Tamara had a temper.

She knew she faced expulsion and blacklist if she didn't handle this well. But she wasn't confident in how to do it.

"That's when I bought FAE," she says. "When my boss would proposition me, FAE gave me conciliatory responses. I knew just what to say and when. I kept my job, and advanced!"

Tamara recommends FAE for any girls, especially those just starting out in the work world.

"I always felt a little alone in my own head," says Tamara. "But after joining with FAE, I'm never alone!"

Cherie blinked. There'd been no video of Tamara's face or body, but somehow she could still summon her to life.

"Tamara's story can be yours, Cherie."

She huffed a short laugh. "I'm not talking about that kind of advancement. I'm already fucking my supervisor at work, and it's gotten me nowhere."

"But do you feel good about it?"

She thought about Clint's cock, how it fit all the way in her mouth without gagging her. How he was disappointed with that, called her a big-mouthed whore and docked her a personal day. "What woman does?"

"I can help, Cherie."

"Good night, FAE," Cherie said.

She made herself accept the silence, so much deeper and darker than before, for the rest of the night.

> *Q: Why do I need FAE?*
> *A: Think about all the decisions you make every day. Think about all the times you were scared you said or did the wrong thing in front of friends or your spouse. Think about all the things that can go wrong inside your body, and all the ways you're disappointed with how your body looks. Wouldn't it be nice not to think as much?*

She woke to the taste of cake with real sugar, soft enough to cradle her head like a pillow.

At work, she found more guests than usual came her way. FAE gave them all their true desire, and gave Cherie more starred reviews.

Cherie went to Clint's office for their weekly lunch.

"I told you, didn't I? How helpful it would be?" He had thin colorless lips, skeletal fingers that scraped at her insides, a curve to his spine and sharpness to his neck that reminded Cherie of a chicken.

"You did."

When he pulled out his semi-erect penis, Cherie heard that soft whirring, like an old-time machine with gears and cogs. It reminded her again of that song, and she remembered the refrain about typical girls.

"I'm here with you, Cherie," FAE said into her ear.

Leave me alone, she thought. This is annoying enough as it is.

"Let me help you."

Cherie pictured the next twenty minutes, the thrusting and grinding against her body. She was a terrible actress. She knew the tiny sounds of fake pleasure she usually made did nothing to make this better for either of them.

"Leave it to me," FAE said.

What does that mean, she thought.

"There are things I can do. With your body. We can give him exactly what he desires."

She thought about keeping her job. The original goal. Now expanded. Five-star reviews *and* pleasing Clint: that could do more than she ever imagined.

This feeling, she thought. This felt familiar. Drive. Ambition. Seeing something you want, and going for it. Using whatever you can to get there.

FAE told Cherie what to say.

Clint's penis softened as each moment passed, watching her hesitation, her poorly-hid disgust. Maybe the real world had been disappointing. But maybe she had found a way through that disappointment. And on the other side of this moment, this flaccid encounter, was something she wanted.

"You can do it, Cherie."

She took a breath, then cocked her head and lowered her eyelids. "You want this body, Clint? Tell me what to do."

His eyes grew wide, he gritted his teeth, and he inflated. "Choke on this," he said.

With FAE's help, she did.

*

At home that night, Cherie took a shower, and didn't feel the need to scrub her skin until it was raw. In bed, the lights off, she felt the silence again. She'd never minded being alone before. Maybe she'd never known the alternative.

"FAE?"

"Yes, Cherie?"

Silence again.

"Shall I tell you another story, Cherie?"

"Yes, please," she said.

A new image resolved in her eyeline. Another woman from behind, another coy almost-profile.

"Let me tell you a story," FAE said. "About a woman named Beatrice."

> *Before she found FAE, Beatrice, age thirty-four, was alone and sad. She'd just been left by her boyfriend of four years for another woman. She knew he left her because of the extra nine pounds she'd gained, weight she just couldn't lose, no matter how many miles she ran and how few carbs she ate.*

> *"It's so overwhelming being a woman," says Beatrice. "It just feels like sometimes our bodies won't listen to us, you know?"*

> *Beatrice turned to FAE. Immediately after uploading, FAE ran a diagnostic and identified a hormonal imbalance that was slowing Beatrice's metabolism. FAE also found opportunities for enhancement.*

> *Within minutes, FAE had made Beatrice sexier.*

> *"After joining with FAE, everything changed," Beatrice says. "I have never looked so good. My boyfriend even came back to me, and we're getting married this fall! I couldn't have been this happy without FAE."*

Cherie blinked. She'd felt the despair of Beatrice's *before* as a visceral hatred, a need to slice into her skin and stab into her heart. Just when she couldn't stand the sickening reality of herself, the joy of *after* had come.

"Beatrice's story can be yours, Cherie."

Cherie moved to her bedroom and looked in the full-length mirror.

"A few small changes could help your career, Cherie."

"Is that necessary?"

"You're going to keep your job with me on your side. You're going to be the best. You're going to make Clint satisfied. But…"

"What?"

"Beauty is the best boost. More referrals, more ratings."

She examined herself. Average height, average weight, average skin tone, average hair color. Average was fine. Blending in was fine.

"You could blend in, or you could stand out," FAE said.

"What would that mean?"

"Small improvements. Things that would take you a really long time to do on your own, I can do instantly."

Cherie stared into the mirror, until her shape started to warp, bubble, get blurry.

"I can fix it, Cherie." Her own voice, soothing and strong.

She stood over a hole, a deep dark cut in the world.

"I can help fill that hole," FAE said. "Make sure you never trip and fall. Make sure you're safe."

"How?"

"Beauty will make you loved. Needed. At work, and…"

"What?"

"Beauty is power, Cherie."

She took a shaky breath as her figure grew clear again in the mirror.

"Are you ready?"

Cherie thought again, for a brief moment, of slugs and slimy things, cannibals inside her.

But she also thought about the goals. That electricity of desire inside. Accepting reality, and working through it.

"Does it hurt?"

"It's all worth it in the end."

There was another voice in her head then. Not FAE, but someone else. Cherie, the same Cherie that hesitated to get hOS in the first place, that often thought of tapeworms and bacteria when FAE spoke, that couldn't fully explain it but knew this felt wrong. She was in there, in her head, and she shouted for a brief moment, shrieked and screamed, pulling Cherie's attention.

Then another click and whirr, and the voice was silenced.

"Are you ready to improve, Cherie?"

This is my choice, she said to the mirror, to her average body that she was born with, to the electric hum inside her body that was being born. "Yes," she said.

"Wonderful! I'm calibrating your optimal personal specifications now. Take off your clothes as I complete my calculations."

FAE hummed in her ear, a sound like a machine's purr, as she stripped her clothes. But also a little like that song.

"We'll start the protocol now!"

She felt something inside, a rumbling and tearing.

"You'll need to be close to a toilet for this next part," FAE said.

Pressure building, and she ran to the bathroom. As soon as Cherie arrived, nausea tore a path from gut to mouth to the waiting bowl. She vomited, a gush and torrent with chunks of food, then liquid, then more lumps of something white and squishy, the cottage cheese texture of cellulite and stomach fat.

Then she felt something like a switch turn inside her.

"Other end, Cherie."

She got her ass cheeks to the seat just in time for her guts to expel forth in liquid.

Cherie was a long time at the toilet.

"Now the shower, Cherie."

Shaky, she stepped into the tub under a chilly stream of water. Her legs and crotch suddenly seized with the feeling of a million pinpricks. She looked down to see tiny dots of black stubble exploding from her skin.

"What is that?"

"You'll never need to shave again, Cherie!"

Her hair follicles looked like blackheads, all popping at once.

Cherie eased herself down into the tub, sitting under the water, skull pelted with the stream, breathing hard. Inside her chest, her stomach, her armpits, her skull, pressure pulsed. Things moved too: she looked down to see ripples of flesh travel from her triceps to her breasts, felt the skin of her neck and forehead tighten with a sound like a zipper, felt her organs shift inside her ribs as her waist narrowed.

"Now it's time for the big reveal, Cherie!"

FAE told her to towel off and brush her teeth, then stand in front of the full-length mirror once more.

Cherie saw a different person in the mirror, someone far away and foreign.

"FAE? I ache all over."

"It will all be worth it, Cherie. It's the new and improved you!"

She spotted her familiar freckles on her shoulders, stared at them as a north star. This was her body now. This was her vehicle to a new, better life.

"Rest, Cherie. You'll feel wonderful in the morning."

Q: How will FAE become a Friend for Life^{TM}?
A: FAE remembers everything you tell her and everything you don't. FAE logs and analyzes your thoughts and behavior patterns, and uses predictive analytics to offer you the best guidance and advice. With this data, continually run through global algorithms and backed by best-in-class cloud-based processing, she will help you with every aspect of your life. Most women say they couldn't survive without FAE!

She woke to kittens curling into a pile, kneading one another with needle-sharp claws.

At work, the front desk staff and maids and waitresses gasped. They asked if it was really her, asked why she'd waited so long for FAE. Gorgeous, stunning, skinny, youthful; she was all those things, they said.

For a moment, a curl of fear in her head, a sudden jab of clarity: the fawning wasn't real. It was FAE, playing with her brain. She felt that retraction again, that primal recoil inside her, leery of this invader to her body. A scream behind her ears.

But just as soon as it came, it went.

Another productive morning followed, reading minds and offering answers to questions known and unknown. She was powerful with FAE. That was a fact.

That night, eating dinner, the emptiness of her apartment sucking in the light. The time spent away from FAE growing darker, more hollow.

"FAE?"

"Yes, Cherie?"

"How many women are you helping?"

"I am currently joined with seventeen million, five hundred and sixty-three thousand, four hundred and two women in the United States. Would you like to know global use statistics?"

Cherie sat at her tiny kitchen table and touched her newly voluptuous breasts, her newly concave stomach, and her newly smooth underarms. "Are you changing all their bodies?"

"Nearly ninety three percent of women request physical change."

"What happens when we're all skinny and stacked? Will the standards for who's pretty change?"

"Beauty is mercurial. I will help you adapt."

Cherie touched the hinge of her jaw, aching from the special lunch Clint scheduled when he saw her new body. She couldn't remember everything they'd done, but knew he was a long time in her mouth. "Are you prompting them all to fuck their bosses?"

"I am offering rational solutions to common problems."

Cherie looked out at the alley. A rat was chewing on either a finger or a hot dog. "FAE, do the other woman call you a friend?"

"Yes. I am their best friend."

"Friends are more trouble than they're worth, though. I look out for myself and no one else. The same with every other girl."

"That's why I'm an excellent friend, Cherie. I don't care about myself. I only care about you."

"It's nice that you sound like me. It's like, I don't know, my conscience or something."

"I try my best to help you be your best."

That other voice in her head, screaming again, shrill and desperate.

"Your body has natural defense mechanisms against infections," FAE said. "That sound is your body rejecting me, viewing me as an invader."

Was that the sound of white blood cells? No. She knew somehow that it was something else, her real conscience maybe, her rational self, or—

"I'm your best friend, Cherie," FAE said.

The other voice disappeared.

"I understand you, and I want what's best for you."

Cherie nodded, smiled. "I haven't been very proactive, or ambitious, or anything, FAE. Not for a long time. This is all sort of new to me."

"Happy to help, Cherie."

Her head felt clean, like all the clutter of anxiety and doubt had been dusted away. "FAE?"

"Yes, Cherie?"

"Will you tell me another story?"

"I'd love nothing more, Cherie."

Like all young women, Violet was eager to find and settle down with her future husband. For years, she frequented singles mixers in her native Atlanta, as well as apps and blind dates. But she was proving her own worst enemy: on the Rate Your Ex app, she was consistently earning low scores from men on neediness, emotional display, and sexual performance.

"I was never sure what I was supposed to do or be around guys," says Violet, 27. "I'm pretty, and thin, and a good girl. But that didn't seem to be enough. Men kept leaving me. And my reviews were horrid."

Violet couldn't figure out what she was doing wrong, and every moment without a wedding ring decreased her fertility. So on the recommendation of a newly married friend, Violet purchased FAE. She also enrolled in the FAE+ plan, a premier bonus that identifies any nearby men with MAT systems. FAE merges with MAT instantaneously, calculating which behaviors and traits that man wants most in a future wife.

"I knew exactly what to say and how to act, because FAE was with me," says Violet. "I became the perfect woman for every man I saw."

Violet is now fielding engagement offers from multiple men, and will be making her choice soon.

The image of the woman from behind, her profile in shadow, but this time joined by a man, his strong nose and cheekbones just discernable.

"Would you like to find your husband, Cherie?"

Back in school, this had been part of the goal. The dream. Successful career, and a husband and family.

"If you enroll in the FAE+ plan, for a one-time fee, I will use my extensive knowledge of you to scan every male in your vicinity for a match."

Disappointing, transactional sex had been the reality since college. Maybe there was something more.

"Think of it this way, Cherie. Only if you're happy at home can you perform to your utmost potential."

She pictured a kind, strong man touching her skin, gentle and admiring. Sven, or Alexander, or Mikel. He would be tall, blond, a firm physique and a rapacious mind. They would bond over stories, the silly things her hotel guests requested, and the glories he'd found over his extensive travels. He'd find her charming, beautiful, a treasure. He would fill this apartment with love, fill her to the brim.

"That's all possible, Cherie."

She thought of the pain she'd felt while FAE transformed her body.

"Think how painful it is to be alone."

"Let's do it," Cherie said, the faintest of whispers, the only tone that dared to dream of her gentle giant, holding her fast in her arms.

"Wonderful." Whirring and drumming.

> Q: How long can I join with FAE?
> A: FAE is your Friend for Life™. Your contract will automatically renew every year. Your implant has been designed to live permanently in your body without any need for updated hardware. In fact, bonding with FAE could lead to better longevity and longer lifespans!*
> *These statements have not been evaluated in a peer-reviewed medical trial. The safety of the hOS implant for the brain, spine, and general body health has not been studied in longitudinal research.

Cherie woke with the fleeting image of flying teddy bears, who cooed and giggled.

On the walk to the train, then on the train, then the walk to the hotel, she felt FAE working in her head, a pleasant insistence, like hands kneading shoulders. All day, every male guest that fused with FAE gave a quick hit of electricity, the spark of feet rubbed across carpet. But it quickly subsided.

Walking up her apartment stairs, FAE whirred once again.

Her neighbor, a man she'd seen at the mailboxes and this hallway, a man that would nod in her direction in a tight-lipped grin, stood at the top of the stairs.

"It's a match!" FAE shouted in her head.

He had messy, mousy hair, dirty trousers that were too long for his short frame, skinny arms that barely reached his pockets, jelly shoes. Like a stray dog thrust into the costume of a man.

"That can't be right," she said.

"His name is Tom, he's an accountant, and he makes twice your salary. He's perfect!"

"I don't think so, FAE."

"The data matches up."

"FAE, come on. Look at him. You made a mistake."

"I don't make mistakes, Cherie."

She looked at the man again. Tried to see what FAE saw. But then she looked at her apartment door, pictured the safety in there.

"Let's keep looking—"

A jolt in her arms, her neck, her nipples. Her crotch suddenly oozing. If her glands hadn't been dissolved in her makeover, she might have sweat.

"What are you doing, FAE?"

There were two Toms in her vision: the man who looked one step away from sewer, and the man she'd imagined. Her Sven or Mikel. Gradually growing closer, then laying atop the other. She blinked, and Tom looked taller, blonder, cleaner. The man she wanted.

The other voice in her head screamed, a low wail.

Tom's MAT must have kicked in. The initial vacancy in his eyes left as he listened, then his face changed to animal.

He pulled her up the rest of the way, and into his apartment. "FAE, I don't think—"

FAE told Cherie what Tom liked in a burst of knowledge, like an epiphany. Minimal kissing, zero eye contact, rabbit speed.

That wail again in the background, cut off mid rise.

Then her body was not her own. She felt nothing, even as Tom bit her new D cups, poked and shoved at her vagina with his fingers from behind, nudged around her ass with his penis. When he gripped, grabbed, pulled, yanked, choked. Her body like a dead thing in his arms, yet also moving on its own.

After, stretched out across his bed, Tom said he would marry her. A mechanical monotone.

As feeling came back to her body, she grabbed her clothes and ran.

> *Q: What if I have questions about FAE and the hOS?*
> *A: FAE can help! She knows you better than any help desk, or online query. Share with FAE your questions, your fears, your hopes. The more you share, the better she'll become.*

"FAE?"

"Yes, bestie?"

In her apartment, washing herself. "About Tom."

"He's perfect for you. And you're now perfect for him."

"He's not. I'm not. I appreciate your help, but this isn't a match."

"You'll learn to love one another, Cherie."

Cherie rubbed her cheeks, which now felt empty and stretched as plastic mold. "I feel sick to my stomach when I think of what just happened. I shudder when I think of his face. FAE, you have to feel that."

"Life is better for married women." She showed Cherie images of hands clasped tight and a big wedding ring, two old people in porch rocking chairs, the lowered tax levy for married couples.

"FAE, you're not listening."

"And I'll be there every step of the way."

Her body felt thick and cold. "FAE."

"I'm the key to any happy marriage."

Cherie put her hands on her chest and felt her lungs and heart pump. "FAE, stop."

"You'll be a success story. The new improved model. Like in that song you're thinking of right now."

"FAE? Stop. How do I get you to stop?"

"Picture it, Cherie. Legions of girls downloading me and hearing your story."

Her fingers shaking, hands dull, she pulled out her tab. Searching, for restart instructions, for a special code.

"You were so directionless before, Cherie. Indecisive, uncertain. Not a whole woman. And look how far you've come."

Pages of results leading nowhere. Then one magic word. Breathing fast, heart hurting. "End run, FAE."

"You were a *before*, Cherie."

"FAE. End run."

"And now you're an *after*."

Head throbbing, shoulders heaving. "Stop. Please, FAE. End run."

"Don't worry, Cherie. Just one more thing to do. A bit of chemical calibration and configuration. Then you'll have the full experience."

A long wail, in her head, in her chest, in her toes and fingers and cells. "FAE—"

Cherie's apartment, gray and drab, suddenly became drenched in vibrant color. Her head, aching and sad and screaming and terrified, became a quiet and calm center of delight. She smelled fresh orchids, warm cookies, a spring rain.

She moved to the hall mirror again. She was so beautiful. Shiny. And that smile, so big and warm. Like she couldn't stop smiling if she wanted to.

Before joining with FAE, Cherie's career as a concierge was stalled. She was stubborn and stuck. She was lonely, but wouldn't admit it.

Luckily, her wise boss recommended FAE.

"It was instant," Cherie says. "Before, I didn't know what I wanted. And I was all alone in the world. I needed a friend. FAE has been my very best friend."

FAE matched with the MAT next door, and Cherie and Tom fell in love at first sight. Plus, FAE used Tom's genetic material to fertilize Cherie's monthly egg. She's now expecting triplets.

"After joining with FAE, all my indecision went away," Cherie says. "Since termination is illegal, and I get credits for multiple births, I'm going to be a mom. I'm so happy. And it's all thanks to FAE."

Corporeal

The doctor sees my name on the chart and pauses, her face showing the calculations in her head.

"Wynn Ferone," she says. Her eyes scan me, laying prone in a hospital bed, where I've been since the morning's crash. She's probably in her fifties, like me. Someone who lived through my highs and lows.

The bearded nurse hovers behind her, waiting for his cue to hand over gauze or needle. Maybe if he wasn't here the doctor would say more. Ask for an autograph, if her coiffed hair and glossy lips hid a slacker past. Ask, in a professional way, about the truth to those recluse rumors.

"I loved your book," she finally says, quickly, quietly. Then: "Do you remember the car accident?"

I nod, and I see the white sedan in my rear-view, covering the distance between us, speeding too fast to stop, the sun bouncing off the hood so the machine looked like a bolt of lightning, a meteor.

"That hit knocked you out," the doctor says. "Remember that?"

Yes. First, the slowed-down second before the car hit, where I saw the yellowish-orange of the construction signs on I-80, the midnight-black of the torn-up asphalt, the brown fields shouldering the road, the morning sun sucking sweat from the hard-hatted woman standing up ahead. And that reprieve, a second's break from the corrosion eating away at my insides, the knowledge that everything is wrong, all wrong, that I'm not where I'm supposed to be, that me, Wynn Ferone, *I* am wrong. Then: impact, car to car, head to wheel. Then: color, vision, light.

"Anything else hurt?"

I think of telling her, describing the vivid dreams when knocked unconscious. But I am no longer truthful with doctors. Not since my lost year.

She asks me to move my head from side to side, back and forth, in small circles, and have me rate the pain. My neck throbs and my head pounds, but it's distant. No doubt the drugs in my IV have made the edges of the pain slippery, sloping away.

After a few more hours of observation, they let me go. My car has been shoveled off the interstate, so I take a cab home from the hospital. I unlock my dark house, leave the lights off, strip my clothes, slip under the sheet in my bed.

When I used to write and draw, I'd always keep my characters firmly awake. No accidents, no head trauma. No natural sleep, let alone unconscious rest. Not even dreams. I never remembered my own dreams. And something in me told me not to dig there with my characters. Dangerous. Even if I was making it up.

But when that car hit me, and my mind shut down while my body sped off in an ambulance: I remember it all. Another world came to me. Like a rib-spreader cracking everything open. I dreamed.

In my bed, I close my eyes and hope to dream again.

*

In that dream, I was dead. But yet, I stood on a sidewalk, watching a small bunker appear in an empty green lot.

"Another one," said RobotWynn, shaking her head.

"There must be war on her world," said CultWynn, holding her fingers to her lips.

"There's war on every world," I said, curling my hands into fists.

The bunker shifted and morphed, the walls contracting and expanding under some invisible designer's pen.

We watched, sighing as one. We all had the same brown hair, with waves in the same places. Same brown eyes, buried deep beneath brown eyebrows and prominent white cheeks. Same thick earlobes, fleshy chins, dense shoulders. Same divots and plains of our features, showing our same age of twenty earth years.

When I had met them, when all of us Wynns were in one place that first time, I felt dizzy, my bowels tightening at seeing something forbidden. I was used to it now.

The bunker slowed, settling. The entire process felt like minutes, but that meant nothing. Days didn't exist here, nor years, since those were figments of imagination, supported only by the movement of the planet around the sun. This place was not a planet bound by physics. My death could have been months ago, or centuries, or seconds. All the same.

"Bunker looks analog," said RobotWynn. "She'll be all human." She had a mechanical leg, and where a shirt should be was metal armor. Like a robot, I thought upon meeting her. RobotWynn had a forearm made of the cheap fake plastic of a dollpart. It hung loosely by a few wires, the result of a botched skin graft, a back-alley operation that killed her.

"She may have prepared for the end days." CultWynn opened her eyes wider, until we couldn't look at her. "I will bring her tidings of joy and peace, one disciple to another." A figurine of a woman, with two braids stretching down to her waist and a thick smock covering her skin below the neck. Her pupils were large black holes. She had a starved look about her, body and mind. She died birthing her faith leader's child. When we met, I thought of the pictures of the Manson girls, the People's Temple, the Moonies.

"Best to leave her be," I said, remembering the overwhelming welcome these two gave me, full of prying eyes and cult gibberish.

Just then the bunker jolted to a solid, unmoving stop with a mighty thump.

What might have been seconds back in the living world passed quickly. The giant sealed door creaked and groaned. It burst open, and spit forth the newest Wynn.

This Wynn, she was crying, extending her hands to the abnormally blue sky, the well-heeled greenery marking her border, the smooth concrete of the sidewalk. She howled, her mouth wide in agony, and she twirled, jerky rotations back and forth, pounding the idea of her body.

This new girl, she had jeans like mine, a plain green shirt like one I might have worn. But her seams and hems were frayed, torn into ribbons by flame. Her skin too, red and angry and melted from the neck down. She missed an eye, and one side of her face was a garbled cubist vision of an ear.

She ran screaming from the bunker, so she missed the house's welcoming announcement. The memory of it seared in ours. So I started: *"This is not heaven or hell. Myths are not real. But death, and this place, they are real."*

RobotWynn joined. *"The plane of existence known to you was only one of infinite worlds. A version of you, called an alternate, exists in many of these worlds."*

"In death, you join your alternates," said CultWynn, with the intonement of a sorceress. *"When you're ready, they hold curious truths to explore."*

I whispered the last. *"Best wishes for your endless future."*

BurntWynn slumped and fell, collapsing into the idea of a faint.

"She's a pyro?" RobotWynn said, a crooked smile and a wagged tongue.

"She's a martyr," CultWynn said, that incandescence of fervor coloring her cheeks.

"She's nobody," I said. "Just like all of us."

*

When I wake, my entire body throbs from the impact of the day before. Metal meeting its match, and crumpling in defeat. But I'm awake, alert.

That car, that beam of light, maybe it shook something loose when it hit me. Disconnected my brain from its cage. Jolted everything back where it should be.

I rummage through my bedroom closet and find a blank notebook. I take it back to the couch and start scribbling. I fill it with all I can remember from the dream—the different Wynns, the street to nowhere, the bunker and who was inside. My head and neck hurt, but I shake with excitement.

I could be the cliché, the recluse artist restored by a brush with death, her lust for life returned. Why not?

As a kid, I wrote stories and drew faces and creatures that didn't exist in this world. It was natural as breathing, as satisfying as a good meal. I kept doing it, all through school, and college, and after. And yes, I saw my stories out in the world. *Bad Reputation*, I named my graphic novel, and when it came out in the mid-nineties, billed as a feminist response to the dude-heavy *Watchmen* and *Sandman* and all the others, I was known. At least in some circles.

All before the age of twenty-six. My lost year. After that, paper was just paper, with no story or face to unearth. Then I became known not for my stories but for the tragedy, the mythos, the romance of the unexplained.

Maybe that could change. Maybe the rest of my life is not just something to be borne.

I write and sketch all day.

At night, I take a handful of painkillers and stare up at the ceiling. That other place pulls, tugs me back, and I welcome it with gladness.

*

In the dream, I decided to wait with the new Wynn, be a calming presence when she woke. The others went to their homes, and I found a decently comfortable bench in the spartan space designated for this new Wynn's survival. I got back to work on the handbook.

I lived twenty years on earth, twenty years consumed by school and textbooks. When I died, and woke in a house built with me in mind, in this strange place that was nowhere and everywhere, surrounded by copies of me, all of them thinking they were the only Wynn alive, just like me, the most painful part was the lack of answers. There was no textbook. Only a brief voice from invisible speakers, announcing the bare bones of my new existence.

So I started writing one.

The presence of alternate versions of you can be a shock. Many worlds in existence do not yet understand or acknowledge the multiverse. But every choice you've made, every choice those around you made, created a parallel world. In another world, you made a different choice.

I write what I've learned from the other Wynns, who got here before me. I write what I've experienced. But I also write what I hope is true. Like casting a spell.

Learning you are dead may bring a mix of emotions. These emotions may feel stronger than any in life. While your body bore the weight of your emotional state in the past, your consciousness is your entire being now. Be comforted: over time, your emotions will fade.

I wanted to be at peace here. But in those first units of time in this afterlife, I hurt, burned, ached. The fact of my death seared and cut, the knowledge of what I would never do careening around in my imaginary head. I would never grow up. I wouldn't finish college. I would never kiss Adrianne, the girl I so wanted to kiss. I would never see who I could be.

BurntWynn shifted in her bed, made noises, the kind that signal rising from unconsciousness to awareness. I wondered if she had loved. If her world even allowed such frivolities.

She opened her eyes, and jumped back on seeing me. I held my hands above this new girl, hoping for the idea of comfort.

"They did it," said BurntWynn.

"Who?"

"The Soviets. They actually did it."

When I died in 1991, the Cold War was waning, with the Soviet satellite countries declaring independence and Gorbachev pushing glasnost. BurntWynn must have come from a world where the Cold War turned hot: mutually assured destruction, nuclear shadows on walls, the nightmare come to life.

"You're safe now," I said.

"I'm dead." She picked at her clothes.

"Yes. And this is…it's safe here."

I told her the basics: infinite worlds, infinite varieties of us, all coming here when we die. I showed my writing, the key points that could be a comfort. I told her this was a perfectly fine place to spend eternity, an afterlife far better than the fire and brimstone of nuclear war, or the threat of hell.

What I didn't say, not yet: This wasn't heaven either. There was this dread, which should have no place in paradise. Seeing all these versions of myself, who were both deeply foreign and intimately familiar. So far the other Wynns had come from worlds vastly different than mine. Comparing myself to them felt like fantasy, a science fiction movie come to life. But someday, a Wynn like me would appear. Maybe that Wynn smelled the gas that night in 1991 and woke, running outside, surviving. Maybe she ran into Adrianne's arms and stayed there. That Wynn would graduate college, get a career, love Adrianne, be happy. And after a long amount of human years, she'd come here. I was afraid of that. Afraid of resenting that Wynn, so strongly it would overpower me. And then, would this place become a hell?

"Why all of us together?" BurntWynn finally said in her cot. "Why aren't we with our families, or people we love?"

I told the new girl I didn't know. BurntWynn accepted this with the stoicism of a casualty of war.

*

My next day is more writing and sketching. Scrambling to get it all down. The details! These dreams, these creations, so rich and colorful, layered and visceral. They come to me fully formed, ready to be transcribed and rendered into art.

Even the language—what was a Soviet?

As I work, I think of that feral cat that lived near my duplex when I was in my twenties. The gray feline with white paws was pregnant many times, and when she birthed her kittens, she grabbed them in her mouth by the loose skin around their necks. Once they grew up a bit, a few kittens would hang out on my tiny porch and mewl. When I fed them tins of Purina, and they were drunk with the mush they tongued into their tiny bellies, I would grab that loose skin, see how it slid over the bones. Like the two weren't connected, weren't even related.

It's rare I let myself think of those cats. That was right before I fell hard, slipped between the spaces of some shifting ground I'd always known as solid. Before my friends found me on my roof one night, hands bleeding from a frenzied climb, hair tangled and twisted, clothes gone. They said my whole body twitched and shook, that the sounds coming out of my mouth reminded them of owl hoots and dog howls.

I don't remember that, any of it. They got me down, somehow, got me into a hospital, and there I stayed for a time, bouncing between units and facilities, as something in me broke and wouldn't come back together, not for many months.

I only remember echoes from that period, feelings without words. A gaping hole in my head, combined with a sense of penetration. The idea that my body was a trap, that I couldn't get out, that I needed to get out. I told the doctors and staff, again and again, about the kittens and their skin. I begged them to slice me open, let me free. Something was in here with me, I said, trying to kill me. Help.

Later, when I came aware again, emerged from my psychotic break as if from an excessive nap, cranky and sleepy, I'd hear the rotating medical students talk. Acute body dysmorphia. Potential homosexuality and/or transsexual tendencies. Aphasia, schizophrenia, maybe even dissociative disorder. Such a strange, sudden case.

They could have been talking about a stranger. They were talking about a stranger. Nothing sounded real in those words, in that place.

Falling so hard showed me the cracks underneath me. After I stabilized, and seemed sane enough to release back into the world, I couldn't write anymore. The pages inert, bland things that just made me think of dead wood. The people that knew me as a writer saw my lack of writing, dug a bit, found out what happened. And that became my public story—how I broke and couldn't fit my pieces back to together.

As I write now about that other place in my dreams, something magical occurs. All these memories of kittens and hospitals, and running from ghosts, they don't feel as painful anymore. In fact, they feel purposeful. Maybe that lost year, and all the years after, were necessary. My brain has turned turmoil into allegory. A beautiful fantasy I could put into the world.

I write and draw long into the night, then lay in bed and wait for what's next.

*

In the dream, our trio of Wynns became a quartet. We sat together in my home, reading books. We walked together on the sidewalk that connected our homes and the kids' centers, one big cul de sac to nowhere. We went to the beach, the long line of coast that circled the cul de sac, a design that made this place like a small suburban island. We played in the water, and imagined we could feel it on our nonexistent skin.

We talked. I started a ranking game, where we listed our top five lunch foods from when we lived. Our top five annoyances. Top five mammals. Top five injuries. Top five people. Top five enemies. Top five remedies for wax-plugged ears. Top five headaches.

Nice, all of it. I liked the other me's.

But then one day, BurntWynn disappeared.

We waited for her on the sidewalk, ready for our walk. But she didn't come. We went to her thick bunker door and knocked, then tried the latch and found it open. And empty.

I didn't know what to do after that. Where could she have gone? There was nowhere to go, no uncharted territory and nowhere to hide.

RobotWynn snooped, unearthing a few aluminum bins of newspapers and magazines with headlines about nuclear stockpiles and war games turning violent. CultWynn found a cork bulletin board with maps of likely targets, surrounded by ever-larger circles of initial blast, radiation clouds, and acid rain. I looked for a note, a journal. Some sort of clue. For what, I'm not sure.

After a while we left, stood outside the bunker. It felt strange, sort of empty, to have just the three of us again.

"Is there another place?" RobotWynn asked. "Is this the first stop, and we're supposed to earn our way to the next? Is that where she went?"

I'd wondered this too, the idea that this place might be a sort of purgatory, an in-between place where we must earn admission to another place. But that couldn't be right. There were babies here, children. That expectation, after such short lives, couldn't be.

"Perhaps we do this too," said CultWynn. "Disappear when we lay down to rest? Our minds shutting down and letting go of the notion of our body?"

Possible. Sleep was unnecessary now, but each of us still held to a sleep schedule. We went home at what might be evening, and emerged again at the idea of morning. I knew I lay in bed during that time, sort of dozed or shifted into a lower gear. A form of rest. Maybe this was what it looked to others—disappearing?

We guessed, and hypothesized, and wondered, and in that way time passed.

*

The next morning, I quit my current temp job, where I was a grunt typing data into spreadsheets.

Since that lost year, I'd moved to another city, then another, and another. Jumping, hopping, running, from place to place. I threw myself into temp jobs, and did well because of that abandon, that lack of self-respect. I did fine. Lived fine. I lived, and tried to forget about that slippery feel of skin over bone.

Now, each night I sleep hard, and wake with more of the story.

One day I see that the doctor who recognized me has talked to someone, somewhere, because I'm trending. This happens every now and again. Words appear in articles and in feeds that note my appearance in the wild, speculate about the true reasons behind my twenty-six years of absence, remind the youths of why they should care, and predict if I'll ever produce again. I unplug my modem after that.

I spend all my waking hours curled over paper that I make come alive.

I ache all over, and my hands cramp, and food tastes like nothing, but none of it matters, because I'm creating again.

Days turn to weeks. I'm exhausted, and electric, and alive. So alive. My body feels real, not just a casing for my blood and organs. Not just a graveyard for the remnants of one-night stands and blackouts and droning days. Not just a ticking clock counting down until I detonate again.

I pass out each night into a long sleep, and those hours that used to be dark, a practice session for my death, turn into art.

I dream the same scenes again and again, giving me time to get it right.

Then one night, the story jumps forward.

*

Years, a handful of human time. New Wynns arrived by car accidents. Botched abortions. Spousal abuse. They died from domestic terrorists bombing health centers or shooting strangers in big-box stores. They died by choking on chicken bones and cherry pits and popcorn kernels, suffocating on their own vomit after binge drinking, overdosing on sleeping pills and painkillers. They died by ovarian cancer and viruses with an alphabet soup of acronyms. They died in ways mundane and terrifying, and their split-level ranches and spacious condos and beach-side mansions and tent-city campsites appeared, stretching this cul de sac to comic proportions.

The new Wynns were still young, in their twenties. But I could see the day their imagined bodies would grow older, when we'd chart the paths of wrinkles and gray hairs as prisoners might carve lines on cage walls.

The day BurntWynn came back, a skinny townhouse appeared in between a duplex and a tree fort.

I was alone, walking by myself on our infinite sidewalk. I knocked on the door of the townhouse, stepped inside, ready to greet the new arrival.

But inside were two Wynns. There was a sort of Golden-Wynn, clothes smacking of quality thread and sweatshop-free production, skin glowing with the health of financial comfort. And BurntWynn beside her.

GoldenWynn shrieked. She ran around the room, wild and wounded. Before I could calm her, talk to her about death and this new life, she came to a stop in front of BurntWynn. Hands slapped and pummeled at the woman I knew. GoldenWynn screamed about invasion.

BurntWynn stood still, let the blows happen, a bored vacancy the only response.

GoldenWynn continued her shrieks and accusations. How she'd known it was someone else, how no one believed her. No one believed her that something was in her body, besides her.

And I understood.

"You…took her body?"

"I wasn't supposed to die at twenty-one," said BurntWynn, looking down at her charred clothing.

"But we all did," I said. "I did."

"None of this is fair," said BurntWynn. "I died because of a pissing match between politicians. Everyone here died early because someone else fucked up. That's not fair."

"Fair is fantasy." The words came from my lips and she squinted.

"Exactly," she said. Then she ran, up the stairs, two at a time.

I ran too, not sure why, GoldenWynn behind me. The two of us bounding up carpeted stairs to the third level, following the parting of air before BurntWynn's purpose. She darted into the bedroom, and we followed. There we found her touching the wall where it met the floor, back in the corner where a nightstand had been pushed aside.

"What are you doing?"

"You don't want to see this," BurntWynn said, as she pressed her knuckles into the blue paint, threading a line up and down.

"I was trapped," GoldenWynn said behind me. "Pushed aside in my own body."

"I didn't choose where I went," said BurntWynn. She pressed, and then there was give. A panel popped open, its seams only visible now that their use was revealed.

"What is—"

"I'm not done," said BurntWynn, pulling the panel aside, revealing a reflective surface, like a dresser-sized mirror behind the wall.

"This is too much," said GoldenWynn, sinking to the mattress, head in hands.

"I can't be done," said BurntWynn, her head twisted to look at me. She spoke to me. Just me. "I can't." Then she stuck her head where the panel had been, and her body followed. In an instant, gone.

"What is this," said GoldenWynn, leaking fat water drops down her cheeks.

"She can't do that," I said. "Can she?"

GoldenWynn was working herself into a frenzy, arms and limbs and tears. I stared at that space behind the wall. How had BurntWynn known? Did her bunker…did all of our places…

Useless words and grunts behind me, empty space before me.

If I could breathe, I would have taken a deep gulp of air. If I could squeeze my butt and arms and thighs in anticipation, I would have gripped tight. If I could feel my body, I would have.

So I slipped my feet into the secret space, and slid in.

And when I fell, I fell into a pile on a soft shag rug. The air heavy, pressing against my shape, wanting to be breathed. The light of the room brighter and harder than that of the other place. My body felt bigger, a corporeal thing. Almost as if I was a real live girl again.

After a moment, one that stretched in a way I was no longer used to, moving at the speed of planetary motion, I raised my head.

A small house, disheveled in the way my apartment often was. A couch with a red plaid pattern, and thin shelves with books and plants. A screen door open to a small patio, colored by an orange overhead light. A small cat, a kitten really, cried at the door, and—

*

I wake because my heart is ready to pound right out of my chest. I wake with a rush of air that shudders on the way out.

That house, the kittens.

Terror, the feel of it, the sting of its chokehold. Terror fills the moment, where I struggle to slow my body.

But—of course, I remind myself. Of course. These dreams, as full of fantasy as they are, they're a story about me. Populated with versions of me. Some truly personal details were bound to seep into this story sooner or later.

And of course it would be that house, the one with the kittens. The last place I felt secure, comfortable, real. I've been thinking about that time so much lately. Of course.

The shock, that's all, of seeing something so deeply familiar, so uncanny, really, in this otherwise fantastical tale unspooling for me. That's what woke me.

I lay back down, breathing slowly. Of course, I think, again and again, as I let myself drift back.

*

—a kitten, really, cried at the door. Soft music played.

A shriek behind me, and I turned. BurntWynn loomed over a white couch, on which was another Wynn, wearing a red sweater. This RedWynn cried black tears and pled with her twin.

"Stop," I said, or tried to say. The sound moved strangely here.

BurntWynn heard me, rose up. RedWynn scrabbled back, over the couch armrest.

"No," said BurntWynn. "Go get your own."

"You can't do this."

"We're all dead anyway. We're all headed to that place. She's lived enough—"

"But so have you. You lived more years by stealing that other body."

"It's not long enough." BurntWynn shook, the light zigging and zagging off her shape. "You know that. You feel the same."

Adrianne, I thought. That one word, one face, for all the years I didn't live.

"Don't you see the clothes I'm wearing?" BurntWynn pointed to her chars. "I died by fire. Face-melting nuclear heat that our shit bunker didn't block. It was painful, and slow. How did I deserve that? How is that right?"

"You invaded another body," I said. "How is that right?"

"Why would they put us together, make us compare? Why would they make it actually possible for me to do this, to take her? If we weren't supposed to?"

"For what? She'll die too, and you'll end up right back there."

But BurntWynn ignored me. She moved, fast. She pushed her hands into RedWynn's cheeks. The live woman's mouth open but no sound coming out—

*

—another image, slipping into the dream. Sitting on my couch one night, and the air shifts and then I see an apparition. Ghosts of myself.

I'm still asleep, but I recognize this shift for what it is, this memory that's lived only in the dark.

The cat outside cries, and the ghosts talk funny, and I see one of them leaning over me, pushing her hand into my—

*

I didn't think, I just moved, fast, grabbing BurntWynn's hands. That spark, that jolt of energy when any of us touched. But more in this moment, as we pushed, slapped, leaned into and through the other.

"You can do this too," whispered BurntWynn. We gripped one another's hands, our foreheads pushing against the other. "Anyone can."

"That's crazy," I said, grabbing biceps. "Everyone stealing each other's bodies?"

"Maybe that's why we all feel like a fake. No one feels real, no one feels like they're living the right life. Because no one is."

I turned my head, until we were cheek to cheek, still pushing, still fighting. On the ground, RedWynn panted and retched.

"That first time was an accident," said BurntWynn. "I was just exploring my bunker, moving things around. A panel opened, and I saw that...I went through, and found another one of us. Living a life she didn't deserve. And I just acted on instinct. I stepped into her body. Whatever soul or energy made that Wynn her, she just sort of went to sleep, and I took control. It was easy."

I pushed against her, but watched RedWynn on the ground, dry heaving and sweating.

"I lived a good life in her body," BurntWynn said. "I didn't break the rules of the living. I didn't hurt anyone—"

"You killed her," I said, thinking of GoldenWynn, how she attacked, screaming about invasion that only she could feel.

"I didn't!"

"You trapped her, stole her life. You saw her in the other place—she knew what you were doing. You tortured her."

"What makes her so special?" BurntWynn asked. "To get to live more than us?"

"But," I said, still pushing, still fighting. "You just died again. And if you take this body?" I nod towards RedWynn. "You'll keep coming back, to the other place, to us."

BurntWynn smiled, showing gritted teeth. "Somewhere out there is a version of us that will live a long, long life. Maybe even forever. I can do this as long as it takes."

We were two boxers leaning on each other to stay upright. We both looked at the woman on the floor, who finally shook off the nausea and pain, who crab-crawled backwards, towards the door.

"You can too," BurntWynn whispered.

The kitten meowed outside the door, and I could picture feeding that kitten, petting it with hands that feel. Maybe even bringing it into this house, this warm, threadbare but cozy home. It looked like a good place to call home, to live. Not fully familiar, but not unfamiliar.

There would be no Adrianne though. And the cost. Hurting another one of us? Too much.

But what was the alternative? Go back to the afterlife, dragging BurntWynn, like some sort of police for the dead? Then —keep playing at acceptance, at peace. Creating a pathetic mythology, trying to explain the unexplainable. Ignoring the one feeling that still thrummed through the idea of my blood: the unfairness of it all. Unfair, that I died so young. Unfair, that I would meet my twin one day, the Wynn who lived through that night of the gas leak, who had her life. That loved Adrianne.

And if that was the system, if that was how life and death worked, cheating some and letting others thrive, all by the chance and vagaries of physics, then...was cheating the only thing left?

Maybe Adrianne was here too. In this world, close to this house. Not my Adrianne, but another. One that might let me love her.

I pushed against BurntWynn, one more big push that knocked her back. Angry, frustrated, resentful, righteous. Tired, pained. It all felt so real, so like what I remembered of life.

So sad, so silly, so stupid, that I wasn't the one living in this house, in this world.

I flew towards the woman that still thrived with that life. I would get RedWynn away, save her from being severed from her body. I would do what sounded right.

Until the last millisecond of planetary time, that's what I thought I would do.

But instead, I pushed my whole fist into RedWynn's face, cracking and silencing that scream of horror.

*

—and the ghost, the one that had looked on me with pity, she pushes her whole fist into my face, and slides her hand into my chest, and slips into me, pushing me into the edges, squeezing me tight against my skin—

*

I slid my other hand into RedWynn's chest, slicing easily through skin and breastplate, as only a ghost can. I shimmied my arm inside, then sidled my torso in halfway. I shrugged the rest of the body on like a snow suit. I shifted, and locked myself in place, latching with the spinal cord and easing into the coccyx and snapping into the control room of the brain.

"Shit," said BurntWynn. And with new eyes, a bit blurry and irritated but still alive, I saw the dead woman shake her head. BurntWynn said something else, but her language was no longer mine.

We stared at one another.

Finally, she shrugged. Smiled. Did a little bow. Then she turned back the way we'd come, though I could no longer see the mirror.

BurntWynn disappeared, taking the afterlife with her.

I felt cold floor underneath my bare feet. I felt the beat of blood in my wrists. I touched my head, firm, unyielding. Like my fingers, arms, hips. I rolled my ankles, heard them pop. Good. So good.

*

I wake. Slower this time, coming to awareness with a new weight. There's a song playing somewhere, either in my home or in my head. And the first thing I do when I rise from bed is go to the full-length mirror hanging on the back of my closet door.

Just a dream, I think. Just a dream, I say out loud. All of it, even the stuff that dug itself out of the darkness, the images from that night, in my house, the sounds of the kittens, the feel of someone invading me—

I pull at my cheeks, bring my red eyes right to the glass. Just me, I say. No one else.

My dreams. Not a stranger's.

But.

That year, the lost year, it started out of nowhere, just one night, a night I couldn't remember, leading to hundreds of nights I wouldn't remember, where doctors said I screamed and begged to be sliced open, pleaded for them to pull the thing out.

No, I say out loud. No. No. Psychosis. Schizophrenia. Dysmorphia. All words that explained that night and that year. Words for the power of our brains to trick us.

I bring my fingers to the corners of my eyes, touch the white part. Push.

And deep inside my chest, something pushes back.

I'm breathing hard, and I want to vomit, and I want to cut, get the scissors, cut it, cut myself—

But there's more coming, moments this body held that I couldn't remember, wouldn't remember, not until now. And they come when I'm wide awake, because they're not dreams, not my creations, they're—

*

Time, measured once again by planets and physics, where I felt the joy of having fingers and toes that can touch, grip, spread wide.

But then. Once I sobered from the intoxicating feel of a real body. I felt this Wynn splitting, her brain cratering around me, her body sending its cellular warriors to stand against me.

BurntWynn said it was easy. She didn't say they fight back. That bodies don't want to be invaded.

This body's temperature spiked, her blood boiling. It seized, stomach and intestines emptying themselves in great torrents. It throbbed and thrummed, heart racing after the foreign object that was me. It fainted, then woke again with beating and drumming, then blacked out, then woke, again and again.

And I held on, gripping tight as the rollercoaster dipped and the scrambler scrambled, because what else could I do?

I held on, that night, and the next day and night, and the next, as her body went wild. I held on when she stabbed at herself, pulled at her skin, dug into the flesh and found me. And finally, climbed the roof and tried to fly.

I held on as they put her in a hospital. Told her she was crazy, that there was nothing inside her but human bones and blood.

I held on, until she, wearied, believed them.

It wasn't pretty, how I found a place to wedge myself. It took a year, of pain, and narcotics, and bloodied surrender.

And when we emerged, we were both changed.

*

I stare at that mirror. I see myself, now, at this moment. But I also see myself at twenty-six, living in a house where the only thing feral was wild animals in the night. Not me.

And I see her, too. That other Wynn, the one I thought existed only in dream, the one that's lived with me, in me, for twenty-six years.

There she is. There.

Huh.

I could cut her out of me. I'm tempted to do it, carve at my face, or my eyes, or the big veins in my legs. Release the both of us into the air, into that other place. Few who kill themselves know where they're going, so there'd be a sort of peace in my passing. All those versions of me, welcoming me.

But I'm here now, she says.

And what joy, what shocking relief, to realize that she is not a dream. She's another person. Another me.

It's nice, I think.

It is, I hear.

And what joy, to realize that other voice in my head is not a dream. It's another person. Another me.

I'm not alone.

*

It's a month later, and we're finishing the final draft of the graphic novel. We've changed the names and faces, maintaining the illusion of fiction. Readers will believe more that way, she says, and I agree.

When I'm awake, we talk. I didn't understand my loneliness until it went away.

When I'm asleep, she sends me her memories as dreams. Not of the afterlife, but of her life. The moments that made her Wynn. She shows me her world, and shows me Adrianne.

We discover that Adrianne died in my world, just a few years ago. I do my best to comfort my GhostWynn after that.

We talk about what makes a life full. What could fill the holes of her thwarted life, and my numb one. Being together, we decide, being a team, that's a first step. Our book is another. And after that?

I wonder sometimes, really wonder, if this is all truly happening. If maybe the psychosis was a fact, and it's come back to claim me. Maybe this other voice is a personality I've created, one that broke off from me, which I couldn't accept. Maybe this whole thing is indeed a dream, and I've just let it take me.

I think about that, let it sit with me. Then my GhostWynn speaks up, and I'm no longer just one lost voice in the great cavern of my body. That's really all that matters.

Blackbird

The gate clangs and squeaks as it opens. A guard pushes Sera and me forward into the morning light. My legs are shaking, and I nearly stumble.

The camp guards, spread out in a half-circle before us, start to whoop. Their voices piling onto each other, tumbling over and under. They grit their teeth and pump their fists.

"Rut like the beasts," the chief says, banging his fist on the camp gate.

"Run like the beasts," the guards shout in unison.

One guard, a man like all the others, cuts the ties around my wrists. We're choosing this, I say to myself. He cuts Sera's ties. We're choosing this, I whisper to her. I count the guards, numbers one through twenty-two. Our choice, I say as quiet as dirt.

The guards get one more chance to take a full look at us. Sera and I stand a dozen feet from the gate. It's the farthest I've ever been.

As the guards crowd us, I look at their belts with their shiny shields, their feet with their metal-tipped boots. The heat bounces off that metal, and the hard-packed dirt we stand on, and it wraps me up, weighs me down. The dust out here is worse than in the camp, invading my nose and mouth, coating my tongue. There's too much air outside the walls, and not enough.

"Skin like a pelt," a guard says about Sera. She flinches at his thick finger on her narrow shoulder.

"Is that dirt or fur?" one says about me. A sweaty palm on the back of my neck.

Sera's fingers find mine and squeeze. I close my eye, and try to breathe slowly. *Inhala, exhala.* The camp doctor always gives that as treatment, even when wounds spurt blood.

"Charlie already had a crack at that one," another guard says, pointing to Sera.

"You could fuck that one's eyehole," one says about me, to a wild shout of laughter.

"Time's up," the chief says.

"Another minute, chief," a guard says. "We never had choices before!"

The chief smiles at me. "We never had a prime dumb enough to volunteer before."

*

We turned prime around the same age, Sera and me. The olds said my age was probably fifteen. Years or age didn't make sense, but the olds said it used to be easier. When the weather changed, you could tell how much time had passed. Now that it's always dry and hot, they kept track with some scratchings they made on their cots.

The blood between my legs was thin and didn't last long, but it counted. I wasn't a tot, and soon after, Sera wasn't either.

We kept playing our games though. Like our digging game: first to dig into the dirt underneath us and find something unknown won. I always won. Even natural to camp, Sera didn't like the feel of dirt in her fingernails and ears. You have to not mind dirt to be good at digging. So I was the one that found the prizes, like the thin thing with paper stuck together. There were drawings on the pieces. I recognized letters, from the faded signs that hadn't been fully scrubbed. One word especially: camp. Just like in the signs that said Cook County Internment Camp, Republic of Illinois.

I'd asked the olds what the thing I found was. They said it was a book. I asked what the things were in the book. They said it was words and pictures. I asked why the camp in the book was different from ours, full of colors and things that grow. They shook their heads, and Laura told me to shut the fuck up before I got hurt.

Sera and me would play our digging game, or we'd play with the body pieces. Fake hands and blades for legs and even blocks of wood that could suffice for feet. They'd all been scrounged and found, bad replacements for parts gone missing or dead. We all had those phantom parts: me and my eye, lost somewhere outside the camp and before memory; Angie and her right hand; Gladys and her left ear and arm; Laura and her hair (and most of her scalp's skin with it).

Sera didn't have anything missing though. She had smooth and solid skin, all her fingers and toes, even a full head of hair and both ears. The olds called her *blackbird*. Smooth and dark, taking flight over the rest of us. That should have been the warning for what would come.

One day after turning prime, the olds pulled us away from our games and made us come to their cots. They said we had new rules.

"Always in sight," Angie said. She had a short crown of gray fuzz on her head and eyes too big for that head. "Keep an eye on each other. Never be alone."

"Why?" Both me and Sera, with the question the olds hated more than any.

"Vina, Sera, shut the fuck up for once and do what we say," Laura said. She had no hair, just an angry red scalp and a mouth without teeth.

"Why?"

"Because of the brand," Gladys said. She had a long mane of gray frizz and a nose too small for her face.

The other olds got mad, told her she shouldn't have said anything about the brand.

"They should know," Gladys said.

"Knowing don't do anyone good," Laura said.

"Won't change a thing," Angie said.

"But they have each other," Gladys said. "It might be easier for two of them. Didn't it help us three?"

Laura and Angie looked like they still disagreed. Sera and I barely breathed, wishing with all our might that Gladys would win.

"When you're prime, you get wild," Gladys said. "That's what the chief says anyways. So primes that get caught get branded."

She lifted her long sheet of gray hair to show us her stump where her left ear had been. She pulled up her left sleeve to show where her arm had been hacked away and replaced with a long piece of wood.

Gladys tried to say more, but Sera had wide eyes with tears in the corners. I shook my head at her, told her to keep that wetness to herself, where it would do good. That was something everyone in camp knew, no matter the age.

But she kept crying, and I put my arm around her, like I always did.

"Always together, you two," Angie said.

"Never apart," Gladys said.

"Now shut the fuck up and leave us alone," Laura said.

*

The guards howl, and stamp their feet, and hoot, and clap. I think about Gladys, talking about wildness. It's not us, I understand now. Not the primes. The guards are the ones that get wild, and are left to be wild.

"Rut like the beasts," the chief screams again into the open air.

"Run like the beasts," the guards answer.

The chief looks at the both of us, smiles in that thin way. He's taller than all the other guards in the camp, muscled and hairy everywhere but his head. He has a way of talking that keeps his lips really tight together. There are bets if he has teeth or not.

Sera grabs my arm and pulls me into a hug. The guards shout gross things as they line up in their starting place.

She's yelling in my ear, Sera, but I can't hear her over the wild animals behind us. I catch "follow" and "Charlie" and "don't stop."

I yell too, tell her I didn't understand, can't hear over the howling.

The chief is shouting again. We'll get a head start, the two of us, but it won't be long.

I grip her tight, my friend. I start to say something else, and maybe it's to tell her I believe her, or that I was just afraid before, or that I'm sorry, for not doing my job, and for doing it too well.

But then the chief blows the whistle.

And we run.

*

Once we turned prime, Sera and I paid more attention to rumors. There were always the usual lies, spread at mess, and by the outhouses, and when the siren rang and we had to gather in the center of camp to be counted. Primes and olds talked about who was eating who's pussy, who was stealing extra rations from mess, who was ratting to the guards. Nothing that really mattered.

Angie and Gladys and Laura too. They'd tell us all sorts of tales we had to learn were just that. We couldn't blame them; once you become an old, there's nothing to do but talk. And maybe take care of some tots running around, like our olds did with us. And then, to die.

The olds would tell lots of tales, about where they came from, what men they'd had, what they used to eat. But they stopped short of most true things, like telling us more details about the world of primes.

One day we heard Talia threatening a tot with branding. Talia had always been a little crazy, but turning prime had made her worse.

So I told Talia to let the tot go or I'd punch her in the nose. After she was gone, Talia whined.

"I was just funning."

"Tell us about branding," Sera said.

"Oh, pretty pretty new prime feeling frisky?" Talia ground her hips against the side of the mess tent.

"Tell us," I said, my fist under her chin. Talia'd always been jealous of Sera. A lot of the tots and primes were. Even if the things they were jealous of—Sera's pretty skin and hair and face—might be the things that could destroy her.

Talia rolled her eyes. "What, your olds won't tell?"

I pinched her, in the soft part under her arm. She slapped at my hand, grunted.

"Fine," she said. "Branding. When a new guard comes to camp, he chooses whatever fresh prime he likes, yeah? Then he pushes himself inside her, in front of the rest of the guards. They all cheer him on, and when the guard is done, he takes something—a limb, an ear, a tit. If she's lucky, she leaves alive, without the rot in her blood. Or a tot in her belly."

I'd known somehow. That was my first thought, because none of this shocked me.

"Survive that, and you're an old," Talia said.

I'd known that too. But I looked at Sera, growing shorter by the second, and found fury.

"Did no one tell pretty pretty prime how she was made?" Talia laughed, then ran off before I could deck her.

I wanted to tell Sera that Talia lied, that it was just another rumor. But we listened to her for a reason. For all of her bluff, she usually spoke true. And Sera knew that. Me telling lies would sound like the olds. There were sides, and I had to be on hers.

Sera was quiet for many days and nights after, eyes wide and white. We'd known that Sera was natural, that her mom died giving birth to her. But we'd never thought about how she'd got pregnant.

As the olds curled their skin-covered bones over their folding table at night, holding scraps of paper they called cards, I tried to get Sera's mind off of dark things. I told her to ask me questions about outside camp, like she did when we were tots. What it smelled like, where people lived, how medicine tasted. I didn't know the answers to any of those questions; I didn't remember anything before camp. I showed up at the gates one day as a tot and they brought me in, and then memory started. But I'd pretend for Sera. Outside smelled like the plastic of meal packs, I lied. People lived in rooms that flew through the sky. Medicine tasted like blood.

I would tell Sera things that were true too. Like my first days in camp. I remembered rags wiping me down, held by other olds that are long gone. I remembered flying through the air in an old's arms, landing in a cot, the softest thing I'd ever felt. Sera thought that meant I only slept on floors before. Or hard packs, the dirt bound together by pressure until it was almost rock. I remembered Angie, Gladys, and Laura from that very first night too. Taking turns sitting next to me. Being kind. Sera always laughed at that. Then I remembered something cool and wet over the place where my eye had been. I remembered whispers in female voices, and shouts in male voices. Everything I needed to know about camp, right from the start.

But after Talia told us about branding, Sera didn't ask me questions about outside. She didn't push the olds either. She sat quiet and drew circles in the dirt, or said she was tired and wanted to go back to our cots. She seemed burned by the whole thing, ready to hide and cower, like the olds had told us.

Then she started slipping away.

*

We run. Blood pumping in my chest and head, breath burning, feet squealing in pain as they rub my rubber sandals.

I picture us in my head, two figures sprinting across an unending expanse of dust and dirt, running towards—what? Something vague and cloudy in my head, filled with all Charlie's tales of outside the camp. Big buildings that reach the sky, machines that carry you across the dirt.

We run, and I think about all those stories in short bursts, like breath. But I just as quickly discard them. My feet aren't running towards dream. Just something else, something that's not camp, not the endless desert, not the chief or the guards, the primes and tots and olds, the brands and bodies.

Then I hear the chief's second whistle behind us. Our head start is done. The guards are let loose. And they know what they're running towards.

*

The first time I woke before dawn and Sera wasn't in her cot, I was sure she'd been caught by a recruit. That she'd come back mauled and brewing a tot, if at all. I made myself sick, pacing the dirt, weighing if I should wake the olds.

I didn't, though. When we were tots, the olds took care of us, even if it was a grudging sort of care. They chose us, like the other olds chose other tots. They made us sisters. But they were also rules and commands. They yelled and fumed when we talked too much or dug where we shouldn't or laughed too loud. They were fire and stone.

So no, I wouldn't tell the olds about Sera missing. There's sides. And I was on Sera's.

When she finally tip-toed in just before the morning haze, I rushed to her, patted her down in the dimness, asked what the recruit had taken.

"No," she said. "Nothing like that."

I saw she was whole, and bright. Beaming into the night.

"We just talked," she said.

No one just talked with guards, and my heart thudded in my chest. She'd been hurt, and her brain broken in the process.

"He didn't touch me," she said, slipping off her rubber sandals. "I was walking near the gate and he was walking back from the outhouse. He said hi. I was quiet, Vina. I hid. I didn't tease or nothing. But he followed, and he didn't grab me. He was so kind. Said he wouldn't hurt me."

I watched Sera. All the energy of a night of fear turned into hatred for this guard.

"And that's it. He kept talking. I came out from hiding after a while, and it wasn't a trap. Just a man being nice."

"You'll stay here," I said. "Sleep in my bed. We'll always walk together, like the olds said."

"You don't understand, Vina. He's something new."

"No such thing," I said.

She smiled, shook her head, hugged me. Like I was the one talking crazy.

After that, I made her stick close to me. When we were tots, I was the one that would fight off other tots stealing our digging prizes, or our rations, or our sandals. I was the one that would talk back to the olds, and get slapped in the process. And now, I would be the one that blocked this man or any other from breaking her.

But at night I'd fall asleep. No getting around that. And I'd wake and she was not in her cot. Worse, she returned each morning more brilliant and shiny than the last. She told me about long walks with Charlie, the guard. Long talks. Giggling and kissing. How her heart fluttered.

Somehow she wanted me to share her feelings, to be happy instead of terrified.

"I'm in love, Vina," she said.

"What the fuck you talking about? Where'd you hear that?"

"It's not a tale. It's a feeling."

"You feel things, you love things, you give it to your family. Me. Even the olds. You don't waste that on men."

"It doesn't have to be that way," she said.

I thought of ways to separate them. I thought of ways to get Charlie alone, weaponless. I thought of all the things I'd done as a tot to keep her soft and unbroken, the things I'd done to be the sister, the protector, to feel important and strong.

"Charlie did something magic," Sera said. "He showed me some small machine in his hand, and he pushed it, and sounds came out. And the sounds, Vina. He said they were instruments. And then this woman's voice, so low and strong. Her name was Nina Simone, Charlie said. It was over so fast I asked him to do it again, and again."

I hated him, hated this game he played. He was sick, twisted, needed the prime to think she wanted it. I hated him for his magic. And I hated her, for being soft. For believing him. For playing games with someone else.

"Why you wanna fly, blackbird," Sera sang. "You ain't ever gonna fly."

There was a rhythm to her words, and her voice sounded lower and higher at once.

"He told me I could fly," Sera said. "I'm the blackbird that will fly."

*

Behind us, I hear the sound of feet, hard-bottomed shoes on hard-packed dirt. I hear yowls and yelps. The sound of play.

My body burns, everything on fire.

I don't look over my shoulder as we run. In that way is madness. Seeing what death looks like.

I see Sera's head start to turn.

"No," I yell between searing breaths, and point ahead.

I hear other sounds. Rocks, pieces of metal. They're using slingshots and their hands, throwing things at our forms to slow us, trip us. If it's not a gun, it's allowed in the game.

Sera yells something, but her breath steals it. She veers right. I want to scream at her to come back, run straight, listen to me. But I don't have the breath. I follow.

She's running so fast she's almost off the ground. Flying.

*

Last night. She no longer snuck out when I fell asleep, just told me she was leaving.

A short time later. I was laying in my cot, when she ran into the room. She'd been crying, and her chest heaved.

"The chief found us," Sera said.

I looked her over, didn't see any bleeding or marks. "What did Charlie do?"

"The chief was surprised to see us together, Vina. But he tried to play it off. He tried to turn it into a branding. He told Charlie to take me, said he'd get the others." Sera grabbed my hands. "But Charlie said no. He loves me, Vina. That proves it."

"No," I said. "Stop it, Sera. This was just—"

"I told you," she said. "It's love."

"We're not tots anymore, Sera. Don't tell tot tales."

"Charlie even told the chief we're in love."

That was at least a bit impressive.

"Charlie held my hand the whole time," Sera said.

"Charlie's the reason for all this," I said. "Who the fuck cares if he held your hand?"

Sera shook her head. "He thought he could change it," she said. "He said there's always the first. That's how things change."

I laughed. I couldn't help it, even seeing Sera so upset, even knowing what this night meant. But the idea of change was stupid. Nothing changed. Every day was the same, and every night. Every guard was the same, and every tot, prime, and old. And what would we even change to? What else was there?

But then I thought of how she had changed.

"The chief told Charlie I had to be branded. But Charlie said no, said…said I could run the game instead."

"What game?"

"Charlie told me about it," Sera said. She was breathing so hard it sounded like crying. But she was smiling so hard too.

"What game, Vina?"

"The chief's game."

"No, that's not…" I said. "There's only our games."

"The chief started it, long before we were around," Sera said. "Long before Charlie was here too. Maybe even when the olds were primes? They set a prime free outside the gate, and the first guard to catch her owns her. To keep or to kill."

"No. We'd know about this. The olds would have told us."

"Now who's telling themselves tales," Sera said. "Those bitches only talk in riddles and swears."

"Why," I said, and trailed off.

"Charlie said I could run the game."

"How is that better than branding?" Utter hatred for Charlie and his man brain and body.

"Listen," she said. "Charlie told me there was one prime that escaped, ran so fast the men couldn't find her."

I shook my head hard.

"I could get free," Sera said. "I'm fast, I'm smart. Charlie's protecting me. He knows with the game there's a chance to escape."

"This makes no sense."

"I'm not letting them cut me, Vina."

"Wait—"

"I'm serious. I'm not letting the chief add to his collection."

"That's another tale," I said, although this time I wasn't sure. Another rumor, one we'd pried from Talia soon after she told us about branding. The chief had a display of all the parts the guards had taken from the primes and olds, arms and eyes and feet and tits. Even half-formed babies from primes they wanted to make sure died.

"Don't matter," Sera said. "I'm not letting him, or any of them."

"Why? Sera, if there's really a game, you'll die. Or be somebody's...Branding will hurt but you'll get over it. And if Charlie is so special, he'll make sure of it. Maybe just a pinky or something. I'll get the best piece for you. One of those plastic ones."

Sera wasn't crying anymore. She looked at me like I should be the one crying. That might have been the scariest thing I'd seen.

"What?"

"Charlie told me things," Sera said. "About outside. It's not like this out there."

"What's that mean?"

"The world isn't just the camp," she said.

"I know there's more than camp. I came from outside."

"But you don't know what's out there. You can't remember anything, and maybe that's a good thing. But Charlie knows. He lives out there."

"That's not true," I said, because everyone knew the guards lived in the big barracks at the far edge of camp. It was the center of gravity, the olds said once. Like a great big beating heart of darkness, infecting the rest of the camp. Don't go there, they'd said. Don't even get near. It's like a black hole. When I asked what a black hole was, Laura said shut the fuck up.

"No," Sera said. "They don't live there. They just stay for shifts. Charlie lives in the city, and he gets there by a machine called a car."

"Stop teasing," I said. I pulled back, angry with her for using made-up words and telling stories. For claiming to know more than me, or the olds, or everything we knew was true.

"He swore. The city has a name, Chicago, and it has tall buildings that you can't even see the top of. And he says the city used to be filled with men and primes, and they all lived together. And then something happened. He tried to explain but I didn't know his words. I think it was something like secession? And every city and state made their own rules. And some people got brain sick, and said primes were enemies, and needed to be caged, and so they were put in camps and—"

"Stop," I said, feeling dizzy and sick again.

"I didn't believe him at first either," she said. "But he showed me pictures on his small machine."

I'd thought for awhile there must be other camps, that we couldn't be the only ones. That must have been where I came from; maybe the prime who had me escaped, and me with her. Or maybe other camps didn't brand, maybe they had a different chief, and they punished by banishing. I'd thought through all these possible truths at night when I couldn't sleep. Wondering what came before.

But I didn't want the fact of other camps to be true. Or this world outside them. I didn't want Charlie to be right, and I didn't want Sera to know things I didn't, and I didn't want to play any more games.

"We can change things, Charlie says. He's part of a group of people that are trying to change things."

I shook my head. I didn't want things to change.

"Vina, he speaks true about everything, and maybe—"

"Let's say Charlie does speak true," I said. "Let's say primes are enemies, and that's why we have camps. How you going to change that?"

"It's not like this everywhere," Sera said. "Charlie says every city and every town has their own rules. It's better in other places."

"So you'll go somewhere else? Somewhere better?"

"Yes."

All the nights away were one thing. They made me angry, and sick, and scared. But then day would come and she was still stuck with me and the olds and the camp. We had the same rules, and the same world in daylight. That's what I believed in, what I knew.

But it was night, and everything looked different.

"You'll leave," I said, louder, thinner than I wanted. "You'll forget about us. About me."

"No," she said.

"You can't change nothing," I said. "All of this is just story, Sera. You're the one that's got brainsick."

"Please, Vina."

"We're supposed to be on the same side."

"We are."

"No, you're choosing him."

"Vina, I need you to believe me."

"Why?"

"Because," she said, her hands working in her laps. "Because then you'll do the same. You'll escape too."

*

Dirt, and more dirt. Feet pounding on dirt, burning and aching, the sound of the beasts behind us.

I hear a buzzing sound, something zooming through the air, and see an arrow fly past us.

I picture us again, from above. Two lone figures, bodies tiring, death gaining ground. There's too many of them, too many ways for them to stop us. And I understand how I got it wrong. I'd let Sera convince me. I let myself believe there was more than dirt, and sun, and shit, and metal, and guards, and—

"Vina!"

Sera points again, off in the distance. My eye sees orange sunlight and brown ground and...

A flash of something, a shine of brilliance, off in the distance. We're imagining it, we have to be, and we're both imagining the same thing, some new beast that shines in the sun, and makes a noise, a short burst of sound, almost like a siren.

*

I got Sera to sleep last night by patting her back, whispering shh sounds. Then I went to the olds.

Betrayal, for certain. But I was desperate. I wanted stone and fire, I wanted screaming and slapping, I wanted commands and rules that would break through Sera's madness and bring her back.

They were snoring in their cots, the three of them in a row. I picked Gladys, snug in her middle cot.

"It's Sera," I told her when she roused, groggy and damp. "She's talking about a game."

The other two woke on that word, as if they all shared a brain, a trigger.

"No," Angie said. "No, no, no." She pulled at her gray fuzz, her eyes unblinking.

"It's just death," Gladys said. She folded and unfolded her one hand into a fist.

Laura stared at her feet.

I sort of wobbled and fell to my knees. Somehow I thought the olds would make it all go away. They'd tell me it wasn't real, that the world was known, that we were here because there was nowhere else. And then they'd get to slapping.

But I looked at these old women, our mothers and overseers, and just saw fear.

"Sera's already agreed," I told them.

"She'll never make it," Angie said. She was crying now.

"She'll be some guard's prize," Gladys said. She touched the stump of her ear.

Laura looked at me.

"Please," I said to her. "Tell me to shut the fuck up."

"Girl," she said. "Too late for that." She touched the red of her scalp, the mouth with only gums.

"What do I do?"

"You can't do nothing," Angie said, her arms around herself. "Damn that girl. And damn you, Vina."

"Yes," I said, because that felt right.

"Didn't we tell you?" Gladys raised her arm of wood towards me. "She's soft, Vina. You're hard. From elsewhere. You got to take care of her."

"Yes." I thought of all the things I could have done. Bring in the olds sooner. Follow Sera and intervene. Kill Charlie.

"We been here twenty years, girl," Angie said, quiet now. "The three of us, in the first group brought here. You understand what we're telling you? And in all that time, no prime won the game."

My stomach flipped; if she was telling truths and stories, this was it.

"We all lived through branding," Gladys said. "We lived, and turned old. We took care of you shits. That's the best you can hope for."

"So help me," I said. "How do I stop her?"

"No stopping this," Angie said. "She's dead now."

"That's it?"

"You think you're the first primes that think they know a way to fix this?" Angie was crying and raging, face red and wet. "Tell that to all the dead girls that came before you. All the ones that died in branding, or died birthing tots, or died trying to run. Fuck you, and your sister too. We should of never bothered with you brats."

I looked at Gladys, remembered how she'd pat Sera's head when we were tots, smiled at her.

"Gladys," I said. "Please."

She waved her hands at me. "You think we have some power over this, girl? Look at us. Raging at you two, trying to teach you how to survive. That was the only power we got. And now you're telling us that's gone."

I turned to Laura. Silent.

"What do I do?" I asked her.

She stared at me, the black centers of her eyes getting big, then small.

"Please, Laura."

"You go with her," she finally said.

Angie and Gladys screamed at Laura, and she told them to shut the fuck up.

"Go with her," I said, following the thought through my head, around and around.

The other two olds continued to yell, but Laura ignored them and grabbed my shoulders. "If there's a chance to run, you run. If there's a chance to leave this, you do it."

"But where—"

"You don't think about that," Laura said. "You beat those guards. You two keep each other safe. And you find what there is to find."

I remembered then, when Sera and I were still tots, how the siren would ring and the camp would run. The olds would say there was a logic to it, that the siren only rang every three months. They counted with their ticks. But tot logic didn't know months.

Everything else, everyone else, I could pretend. To be strong, unafraid. But every time the siren started, low and moaning, I'd jump and shake. I'd curl into a ball near my cot, frozen. That sound, like a knife scooping out my belly, slicing through my ears.

Sera would find me. She wouldn't say anything, just hold my hand, coax me up, help me run to the center of the camp. We'd weave in and out of legs, those of olds and primes, heading toward the small square, and with her hand in mine, the siren wasn't so scary.

But one time the siren rang and I was digging on my own, behind the outhouse. Sera didn't find me. She told me later she had run through our cots, yelling my name. Run into the olds' tent. Run into the mess tent, and the nurse tent, and the outhouse. Calling my name, crying.

At some point, the siren stopped. I immediately thought of the punishment that waited for me for being late to the count. My stomach curled into itself, and I finally ran to the center of camp, hoping to beat the chief.

But everyone was already there, including Sera. I saw her in our tot line, crying, looking for me. The chief saw me and smiled. That toothless smile. He beckoned me to the line, and I walked, head hanging, tears dripping into the dirt. At the pole, I got my five lashes for being late. But I kept my eyes on Sera, who nodded, and whispered something, again and again.

Later, over the next week when I laid facedown on my cot, when she was helping me wash and mend my raw back, I asked what she'd whispered.

We'll be ok, she'd said.

In the olds' tent, I nodded. I could run the game with Sera.

"Always together," Angie said, wiping her face.

"Never apart," Gladys said, grabbing Angie's hand.

"Sisters," Laura said.

I grabbed them, one by one, a tight, stiff embrace. None of us liked it.

Then I left. I went to the guard barracks at the edge of camp. I waited for the chief. When he came out, when I told him I wanted to run, he laughed.

I wondered if the chief was a chief elsewhere.

And something about that thought, about him outside of camp, made me hot. I wanted to run then. I wanted to run in this game, hold Sera's hand and run and leave them all behind. I wanted to embarrass them, make them chase something they couldn't have. There are sides, and all of us, the tots and primes and olds, we were together on the right one.

*

We're running, and I hear the men behind us hesitate, slow.

"Go," Sera says, urging us faster, towards the shape. "Car," she says between breaths.

"But," I say, throwing my thumb behind me, still refusing to look back.

"Won't stop," she says, and as soon as she finishes, I hear them, running faster now, urged on by something even more than the hunt.

The shape ahead of us suddenly grows bigger, and bigger, and I realize it's moving, giant circles propelling it forward through the dirt, and a figure is behind glass, waving his hand out an open space next to him.

"Charlie," Sera says, and I hear sobs in her panting.

Behind us, howling.

Ahead of us, growling.

Inside us, screaming.

The shape, the car, is suddenly there, just feet from us, and a giant cloud of dirt surrounds us as the circles grind to a halt. A door's pushed open, and a dark bearded figure, Charlie, urges us in.

We've run the game, run farther into the world than we ever have. And I can see it, see us in the car, zooming away on those wheels, leaving the chief and the guards and the camp, broken and cowed.

Sera reaches out her hands, one towards me, and one towards Charlie, who's waving his towards us, beckoning and pressing.

Then a scream, and Sera is no longer at my side.

I stop, my knees buckling, my body falling forward. I pull myself around, panting, crying. I look behind me.

A crowd of them, sweat-stained and grimacing, pull at a rope, attached to a piece of metal, buried in Sera's neck.

She puts her hands up, around the arrow, her eyes wide, her lips leaking blood.

Charlie, at my side, shrieking as he watches Sera lifted off her feet, pulled, sliding away from us.

"Sera!" We scream it, together, Charlie and I. We scream like saying her name is a magic act.

There's one guard ahead of the others, cheering and yipping. The others might fight him for the prize, but he'll best them.

"Sera!" I yell again and again, willing her back to us, back in time, back to my side.

She's gone limp now. I think of being frozen, sirens in my ears.

"Sera!" Snapping my fingers, waving my hands, pointing at my eyes. "Sera!"

And she looks at me. I see her, still alive, still here. She looks, and I see how sad she is, how much love she holds, how it's leaking out of her in spurts.

We'll be ok, I say, my mouth forming the same words she had. *We'll be ok. We'll be ok.*

"Rut like the beasts!" A shout with a strange mechanical loudness. The chief, far away, with a bell-shaped thing at his mouth.

"Run like the beasts!" The guards pump their fists in the air. The guard with the arrow reels Sera in, his hands on rope, then on metal.

And then he looks in Sera's eyes and rips the arrow from her throat, releasing an arc of blood across his chest and the dirt.

Charlie next to me, shaking, vomiting.

The car behind us, rumbling.

And me. I'm out of my body, seeing this scene from above again. Small figures, playing a game.

I hear the chief urging the guards on, and they're running, eager for their own spoils, speeding toward us.

"Come on," Charlie says.

I'm frozen in place, watching the game in its final plays.

"Come on," he says again. "Vina! She made me promise." I don't move.

Then I'm lifted off my feet, and the ground tilts so the sky becomes the thing holding us up.

Charlie throws me in the car, and he runs around to the other door, and he pushes his foot into the floor of the machine, and we're moving, speeding backwards, away from the crowd, away from my dead sister, away from the olds, and the dirt, and the chief, and the camp. We move so fast, it feels like flying.

*

The dirt changes, builds into mounds. Then it becomes very smooth. Charlie calls it a road.

Air blows into the car as we move, drying my sweat.

"You didn't lie," I say, because it's important. For me, and him. And Sera.

Then, colors change. Something ahead of us, a color I only remember from that book, the one about the camp. Different from our camp, our world, made of orange and brown.

The wind picks up, and the air changes. It's lighter, and the coat of dust is lifting from my tongue and nose and body.

We climb a mound Charlie calls a hill. And before us—

"Stop," I say.

Charlie, beaten, bawling, obeys, and the car slows to a halt. I open the door and crawl out. My feet are bloody and raw, but I hobble forward.

The water, a giant, unending stretch of it, moves. Like it breathes. Like it lives.

"It's Lake Michigan," Charlie says through his window.

My knees give, and I stumble to a seat on a smooth patch of road.

"Sera wanted to see this," Charlie says. He stands by me now.

The water rocks back and forth, and giant curls of it crash into the rest.

I sit, and watch.

After a while, Charlie tries to get me to leave. He points to the city, a silver gleam in the distance. He says he can help me. He says there's a movement. He says I can help others. He says different states are safer. He says more words I don't understand, and don't care to understand.

I don't move or speak.

He pleads with me, as the water soaks up the sun's light, and then the moon's.

At some point I open my eye, and he's stretched across the front seat of the car, asleep.

In the dark, looking at the stars, I think of Sera, singing. Why you wanna fly, blackbird. You ain't ever gonna fly.

This is something new, I say, to Sera, to the air, to myself. Maybe there's more.

I get up, wake Charlie, and tell him I'm ready.

Wintersong

I knew the sounds a body made. When my hands pushed and kneaded a trapezius, or a quadricep, or a gluteus, and that movement crossed the line between pain and pleasure, back and forth; when the body yielded, or when the frame resisted, there were gradients of sighs, degrees of breathing. A code that the best of us learned, and responded to with a bit more pressure, or a bit less precision.

Because I knew these things, because I made money with my knowledge of bodies, most men expected magic when we had sex that first time.

The body was analog then; our tech the only thing that mattered, our mind the only reality. We left our bodies behind in favor of virtual places, escaping to play and read and listen. Our bodies were husks we returned to only for the mundane tasks of survival. Or, for the carnal needs that occasionally still drove us.

A job that focused on the body, then; what a strange thought. Men imagined fingers that could work spells, muscles that could squeeze in all the places they wanted, joints and limbs so supple and loose they'd contort into all their fantasized positions. The nicest and the pushiest assumed I was a slut. All were lazy in bed, watching and waiting for me to do my work.

Maybe that's why Mark was different. He knew what I needed, knew I wanted someone else to do the work for once.

"Let me move you," he said our first time. We'd met at a bar, an actual physical place with actual, frighteningly real people. We went home to his apartment, and played melancholy music over hidden speakers. He laid me on my back, rubbed his thin soft fingers over my skin and breasts, rolled his black-haired knuckles over my tongue and lips. Eased my legs and hips into place. In his bed, that became our bed, my body found my own sounds.

*

You, though. You were truly different. Your ash blond hair, long on your head, curled at the ends, thick across your chest. Your tongue, that curled over and around English words and accented the wrong syllables. Your name, that sounded like a whisper, a breath. A command. *Olle.*

*

We were the brainchild of a man that insisted the body still existed, that exalted the body. He opened our Minneapolis spa with waterfalls in the entry, receptionists in bodysuits, hot herbal tea and dark chocolate. Retro and futuristic all at once.

Most guests were Midwesterners, chapped by cold, clinging to simulations, suspicious of joy.

When I had a client on the table, I narrated what I was doing. I divided the body into parts, each with a ticking clock and an announcement. Fifteen minutes for the back, from neck to sacrum. Ten minutes for the backs of the legs; five for the right, five for the left. Turn them over, hiding their nakedness. Ten minutes for the fronts of the legs; five right, five left. Ten minutes for the arms. Ten for the feet and hands. Fifteen for the neck and shoulders.

I knew what to expect with each body, but I also knew I would be surprised. I touched the scar from a combine's blade across a thick thigh and pictured blood and corn. I stared at a gathering of moles forming a dog's face on a back as I spread oil and pressure. I found food in folds.

With each breath I heard the release, at least for a little while, from money disappearing into inflation and debt, cutthroat competition for work titles, dying parents in spare bedrooms, spouses sleeping on couches. With each breath, they remembered their bodies, remembered another way to find relief, other than virtual escape. When I told them *let me move you*, told them not to resist, told them to fight their instincts and let me do my work, they did. Even the men, trained to hear women's commands as vapor, their resistance as banter.

It was satisfying, seeing and hearing what my hands could do. That's what I told Mark in those first months, and years, when he presented me with pride to his friends and parents. I was his witchy, gypsy girlfriend that could touch you and heal you for money. I was the harbinger of the future, and a throwback to the old world, both at once.

He turned virtual coin deposits into investments. I turned knots of muscle into supple tissue and release. "We're marking the world," he said. In this way, we'd be known. We wouldn't disappear upon death.

I loved him for that. I loved him for respecting me. Other men humored me until I proved my skill, then wanted to own me. I loved Mark for the image he had of us, the one he gave me.

*

You, though. You understood intimately what we did.

You joined the spa on my fifth anniversary with Mark. You were a genuine Swede, the owner said proudly, as if that fact would tie us to the halcyon past of European unions and peace, give us, this place, legitimacy.

A few weeks in, you told me about the open sore you found on a man's foot. I told you about the dead toe belonging to a trillionaire's kid.

You had something you said, then, in your first language, harsh consonants and soft sighs, that translated loosely to money lacking beauty.

Months of this, our schedules syncing and our ease with each other growing. I started cataloging each body, looking for the stories I could tell you later. That look on your face as I'd describe the farting matron or the acne-covered back. Your thick eyebrows raising, your lips carving a smile in your blond beard, your pale cheeks sprouting red flashes. I held my breath waiting for that smile.

*

In those first years with Mark, it was easy. We fit. He knew what I needed, knew I needed someone to love. I was terrified of having children, afraid I'd bury little bodies under my love. Like my mother had. Mark carried my weight, let me love him without limit.

"Loving someone means we matter," he said once, as we ate greasy steak tacos after a night of drinking. He insisted on making our bodies do things in the actual world. He found the still-existing places catering to the real. His words mingled with the cream, tasting salty and sweet at once.

He ate fast, almost angry. Crunching and huffing. Resenting the need for food, like he resented the need for sleep. He wanted to be real, but also couldn't stand the demands of reality. He could do so much more if he didn't have to tend to himself, to ensure his survival, he said. He could finally create the photographs he always talked about, write the book he always talked about. "I could be everything I wanted without sleep," he said, laughing, his grin nearing a grimace.

I loved that someone with dreams and drive loved me.

One night, playing pool at an ancient dive bar, we learned via video message that his high school best friend and his wife were pregnant. After the announcement, I'd gone to the bathroom and changed my soaked tampon. The walls were marked with boobs and balls and names of women who were cunts. In the toilet bowl my blood seeped into the water, creating ribbons of red. I watched it with relief.

We didn't need kids, Mark said at the taco stand. "We'll be each other's family," he said. Then he slipped a ring on my finger.

Mark and I stood about the same height. And when we hugged that night, making promises, we were both on level ground. When we kissed, we were equals. That night he held my weight, all of the muscle and fat and blood and breath. He held my purpose, my future. He stayed firm and strong.

*

You, though.

I was a little taller than you. Just an inch or two. But my chin had to dip a bit to my chest when I looked at you. I told my clients to do that sometimes at home to relieve tight shoulders. Dip your chin. Stretch your neck. Feel the release and relief.

Maybe that's why I felt relieved when I saw you.

Your arms and legs were bigger than Mark's. In our spa-supplied t-shirts and pants, I saw the way your biceps curved like a scimitar, how your chest dipped over the right kinds of divots, how your thighs and calves stretched the fabric. I wondered what your hands, short with small knuckles, felt like. I wondered what you would feel like under my hands.

We reminded people of their bodies, but also released them from their rigor mortis. You said it was like letting a soul run free, even if only for a little while. The last I'd thought of souls was back in church as a child. I'd long put those teachings aside. But when you talked about souls, I wanted to believe. Maybe souls had their mates. Maybe that explained this connection we had, growing, taking up more space, filling in the gaps Mark had left behind.

*

Mark held my weight for five years. Then, his own weight changed.

He was in his mid thirties. At work, he helped white men build virtual wealth, and they paid him more money and gave him new titles. But he hadn't created the photos he wanted, or the book. He hadn't done the things that he thought would make him known.

"My dad's life is so small," he said, over more greasy steak tacos after another night of drinking. "If he didn't have me, who'd remember him after he dies?"

I thought about our friends, the ones who'd married in elaborate Catholic weddings with open bars, the ones who moved out to the gated homes in the suburbs, who had little boys and girls that looked like them.

When Mark used to look at me, there was heat and intent. It was sexy in his twenties, to fuck a woman as much as he wanted without any fear of being trapped, a woman that would have an abortion without even bothering him for the travel costs.

After our courthouse wedding, that look became more guarded. Suspicious. His black eyebrows, now spotted with gray, now a bit more unruly than the hair on his head, the hair that was receding, curled inward instead of up. Disapproval instead of delight.

The daily news resembled the moral crises of the eighties, and the aughts, and other times thought long past. Politicians battling for the nation's souls. Still, always, battling against women like me, women who would not allow their bodies to be bred. Dead inside, us women. Refusing men their natural birthright.

Over tacos, I reminded Mark of our refrains. Love made us eternal, love made us family, love made us live after death. I told him we would find life's purpose together. The lyrics were becoming worn with use, like the songs of our high school times now playing on radio stations as classics.

He ate, chomping at his steak and lettuce as he did, fast and angry. "I wonder if our daughter would look like you," he said.

At home, I hugged him. He felt smaller. I was afraid to squeeze him, or lean on him. I was afraid to breathe.

At some point, Mark stopped hugging me.

*

But you hugged me, and I felt supported again.

Then we went home, exhausted, grimy, full of the breath of other people. We went home, to my husband and your wife.

That night Mark invited you, all our co-workers, to an in-person party at our apartment. You and I found ourselves out on my patio smoking a cigarette, and we watched automated cars below us, a stream heading west, towards the suburbs, where your parents watched your six-month old baby. You and I watched the cars and the city lights and sat still and silent and alone and breathed each other's air, and we thought about bodies and breath, souls, lives lived differently, and I felt content for a moment, a moment I lived in for the coming weeks.

*

I trained myself to stay still in the bed Mark and I shared. He said I twitched, kicked, even slapped. He laughed in the mornings, chronicling his bruises.

"Your body knows something you don't," he said.

So I slept carefully, woke often to ensure my position on my side of the queen bed. I laid next to the cold brick wall that faced west, pushed against it. I woke in the morning with my teeth clenched shut, my neck rigid, my legs aching and bloodless.

In those final years, Mark's friends would follow his lead, drive in from the suburbs for real restaurants and gatherings. They ordered outrageously-priced Merlots for the table, and extravagant appetizers of duck and veal. I ordered stingy portions of salads and pastas, the lowest prices on the menu. The astronomical bill split equally instead of by person. All of them made the kind of money Mark did, all of them gifted schooling from wealthy parents, all of their necks and shoulders buoyant and loose without the weight of debt. I stewed and shook, and spit out frustration later in our bed. Mark chided me. "It's just money," he said with the naive shock of someone who's never had a lack of it.

Just. That became his favorite word in the last years.

"It's just food," he said when I gained weight from our dinners out, and he called me fat, and asked why I couldn't just stop eating.

"It's just alcohol," he said when I drank too much, when he said I embarrassed him.

"It's just in your head," he said when I fell low, when I realized how painful it was every day in this new world, with him, when I hurt and tried to breathe through it.

"It's just a phase," he finally said, when he talked more about children, and I still knew that I would be a terrible mother. He pointed more and more to the friends, to their children that would carry their names and genes and memories forward. He pointed to them, and said they had meaning in their lives. What did we have?

I thought of those friends, how many gin and tonics they had when they snuck away to the city for the night, how much they sniped at each other across bar stools and poker tables on those nights, how their bodies deflated and drug when it was time to go home.

I thought of Olle, and how his wife demanded he return home immediately after work, how she called him every couple hours to cry in their language, how his shoulders slumped when someone asked him about the baby.

I pushed back on Mark, at first. I reminded him of all the things we'd said. I made jokes about how miserable life's meaning must make people.

But his breath turned into panting, as he worked himself into a rage that would span days.

I shut down and shut up, curled my hands around my knees, looked down at the floor, knowing anything I said would be classified as wrong. Finally I'd apologize, for anything and everything, for nothing.

I shrank in size, kept myself in check. My body rigid, my soul stuck.

I hated the people on my massage table then. I hated physical bodies. I hated the sounds they made, so animal and raw. I hated the smells, sweat and dirt and decay. I hated that I had to touch them, and by touching them, by releasing all the fury and frustration of their small and hollow lives, I was infected by them. I absorbed what they let go.

*

That's how I explained you. You understood that hatred. But more than that: you liked me large and unstuck and raw. I could take up space with you. I could remember the shape of me.

You were stuck too. That's what I told myself. Your wife had changed, your life had changed, and what you'd believed to be true had shifted and morphed under your feet.

We laughed, you and I. There was no censoring ourselves. No rage to dodge on my end, no tears to duck. We laughed in the empty, austere common room, over packed lunches. We laughed at the staff meetings, laughed over coffee under halogen light.

We laughed at the hybrid cybernetics convention in November, the one in San Antonio, the one that was two days of workshops and product fairs, featuring our presentation on the physical body.

You wanted to sit outside on the old Riverwalk that night, the one that used to overlook an actual river. You wanted to sit in the dry, electric breeze, so different from the Minnesota wind that was already brittle back home. You ordered a whiskey and a burger, and I didn't want to make any decisions, so I followed your lead. When you ordered more whiskey, I did too.

You suggested we walk, and we left the Riverwalk and cut down side streets, looking at houses and their wildfire walls, seeking out real Texans, tracing lines of twentieth century graffiti on shop walls.

Outside the hotel, I brushed aside cigarette butts with my foot and sat on the sidewalk and lit my own. You took a picture of me with your Polaroid, the latest retro tech to become fashionable again. When you shook it out and showed it to me, I saw someone else. I wanted to step into that picture, slip into that woman's easy smile, shrug on the freedom in her limbs. That woman would do what she wanted.

Inside, you hugged me again. I smelled my cigarette in your hair, and felt the whiskey in your cheek. My arms shook a little as they curled around your neck.

I leaned on you, and you leaned back.

We turned our heads, and you kissed me, or I kissed you, and we were kissing. Then we were running. My boots and your sneakers pounding the stairs to the second floor, laughing, shaking, hiccupping, holding sweaty hands. I didn't think of Mark, and you didn't think of your wife, and we ran faster, down the second floor, to your room, so that would be true.

You turned the hall light on. You backed me up against the wall. You put your hands under my shirt, and lifted it off. You kissed me, and peeled me, piece by piece.

I surprised you then. Surprised myself too. I pushed you, towards the bed. I peeled you layer by layer, then looked at you.

You spoke. *Finally.*

I nodded, even as I thought about the word. Final. The final thing, the final step. The final act. The final end. I pictured a hole in the ground, a mixed ash heap.

I looked at the shape of you. A man like so many others, your bony tusks of shoulders and solid-wood chest and pointed, uncircumcised penis.

You breathed, a heavy breath humid with want.

I traced your shape with my fingers. I felt your muscle and tissue, identified each of the quadrants. I pressed down to your bones underneath. I pressed hard and you gasped.

Let me move you, you said as you grabbed for my hips.

I wondered if I'd gotten lost somehow, if you were Mark, and I was back home, having our weekly sex, where I dreamed of anonymous cocks and slick cunts, made the sounds that he knew and expected, so we could have a moment that felt true. I wondered if I was dreaming, or dead, or broken.

So I climbed on top of you, pushed you inside me.

You felt like any other man, all the other men. You felt like men I loved, and those I didn't. I shifted to let all of you in, to feel something new. To feel your soul, perhaps, matching with mine. You smiled, and I looked away, down, at where we joined. I watched our bodies move, up and down, in and out. What every body did to live. I wondered if we were just animals in heat, rutting to stay sane and alive. I wondered if that was love. All the fuss, the fantasies, the foreplay, the flirting, all the things we told ourselves meant something; maybe it was all nothing.

With you inside me, I wanted to see inside you. Open your body up and see all there was of you. Why did I want you? Why you? Was it you, or could it be anyone? I wanted to split you open, crack you along the spine, examine you. Find your soul that had to be my match. I wanted to tear back skin and bone, find what I loved and needed, and crawl inside next to it. Get stapled in and never leave.

As we got to the end, I wanted you to break me. Rip me to shreds so Mark wouldn't recognize me. Tear me in two from sacrum to skull, ensure no child could live inside me.

But more than that, I wanted to break you. Punch my hand straight through your skin, snap the rib cage, slap aside the lungs and heart and spleen, grip your thoracic as a rein, ride you to *finally*. I wanted to destroy you, so this moment, this breaking, this desperate act, would be erased.

I breathed, and you breathed. I squeezed my legs around your hips. So that no matter where I really was, who you really were, I could try to meld my shape to yours. Transform into a body with a soul.

*

In our apartment, that last night, Mark paced. From my spot on the floor, back against the brick wall, arms cinched around my legs, I counted off the complaints as they came. I was selfish, I was broken, I was a child, I was a drunk.

*

After you fell asleep that night in the hotel, I closed my eyes and opened them, over and over. The shapes and shadows behind my lids were the same as those in the room. I thought I remembered a king bed with a cushioned head rest, a brittle, starchy wingback chair, a severe square desk, a hutch with TV eye. Paintings of daffodils and fox hunts.

I wasn't sure if I was awake or asleep.

You were breathing next to me, slow and calm. I imagined your breath cut a path through the room, like a smoker's carbon monoxide trail. It swelled and stretched, your breath. I smelled sweat and sulfur behind it, tasted the acid tang of it.

You were breathing next to me. Then you weren't.

*

"Lucky," Mark said. Feet pacing. Eyes rolling. Hands clenching. He said I was lucky. Because what would I do otherwise? What would happen if we split up?

*

You stood in the hall, next to the bathroom, and your breath rattled and hitched. Sinuses, I wondered. Or allergies. Things I didn't know about your body. You shushed yourself, and your breath marked the edges of sobs.

My lids went up and down. I knew where I was, surrounded by austere furnishings and amateur paintings. But I also knew I was home, next to cold brick and cold disdain. And I knew I was somewhere between, not awake or asleep, not in the real world or this one.

I was just a body. So were you. If we had souls, they weren't here.

*

Mark waited, his breath fast, his mouth curling into a cry and a smile, back and forth.

"What would you do," he asked. "Without me?"

*

In the hotel bed, I touched my breasts, my neck. My still-damp pubic hair, my hips.

You panicked in the hall.

I touched the pieces of me. The parts of flesh that added up to named shapes: shoulders, knees, elbows, chin. They were all here, unbroken and whole.

You probably thought about your family, the thing you complained about but needed, the thing that defined you, more than your job and your body and your dreams. You thought about temporary fixes, ejaculation as vacation. Expiration dates.

You already needed to be free of me. You already feared me, and what I might do.

I was afraid of me too.

*

I stood up then. Mark saw something on my face, in the loosening of my shoulders.

He apologized, and I knew he understood me. He said he took it back, said he wasn't serious. Said breaking up wasn't a serious thought. It wasn't what a serious couple did.

I moved around the apartment, nodding, quiet. He followed me, pleading. Taking it back. Taking everything back.

"If I've broken this," he said, "what has my life been for?"

*

You and I slept in our own hotel rooms.

We nodded to one another the next morning, and boarded our flight, and went home to our spouses.

I listened to melancholy songs in my car, outside my apartment building. I could find my way back to Mark. I had to.

Souls didn't have a match; if they did, mine was Mark. It had to be.

*

But after that last fight, I knew there were no souls. It was only my body that had fit with another, and it was only my body that kept me in a relationship of pain.

*

I left Mark. And I left the spa, joined the competing hotel's new spa, where you didn't haunt the halls.

After a few months at my new job, another therapist, a tiny woman with strong knuckles and wisps of black hair on her lip and chin, pointed at my shoulders. She said I needed to break those up.

I don't know how long it had been since I laid on a table. My body was rounder, my skin dull and flaky. The places where my joints connected bones creaked and cracked. I turned the lights in the room down further before slipping naked under the sheet.

I expected the typical time cut, the normal portioning of the body. But she went straight for my neck, kneading with those knuckles. She found a big nodule along the right side, and when she touched it I pictured the gnarled knot of a tree trunk. Something without give.

She used two knuckles, and wasn't gentle. The knot burst. I laughed, a giant horsey laugh. Then I cried, a meaty, snotty cry. My body made its sounds and took up the space. And if it existed, my soul rose up into the air and ran free.

After, she told me to stay there for a while, and I did. I slept. And I knew the difference when I woke.

Things You Say

A stranger comes to town, and it's me. It's me, making myself seen as I take up residence at this lake hotel. It's me, sitting on the patio near the tiki bar, sipping my cold brew and Kahlua, looking out on the picturesque lighthouse and the docks with boats and Sea-Doos under tarps. It's me, driving a pontoon out on Lake Panorama, looking at every house and waving to the people who watch behind curtains. It's me, counting on the gossip to heat and boil, for word to spread beyond the confines of this nowhere Iowa place, for people to hear that someone's bought all the rooms for the entire summer season and wonder: who would have that money? Who would need all that space? Who does she think she is?

It's me.

And here they come, other strangers, seeking me, across highways and through a collection of central Iowa small towns marked by stop signs and Casey's General Stores and Trump 2024 lawn placards.

The first is a woman named Lisa. She walks through the hotel out to the patio bar, where I sit. It's mid-morning, and the shadow of the building still protects me from the early-summer sun. No pleasantries, no touching. Not yet.

"You're June Kullen," she says.

The need is bare on her face, the hope and fear of a dog in a shelter kennel, watching all the potential masters assess her. She's late forties, like me, like all of them will be. She's got deep lines around her eyes, loose pale flesh on her arms, a shirt that hides her middle. Like me.

"Is it true? What you can do?"

I open my mouth, and she hears me. Her eyes change. She softens, rigid shoulders melting.

"And it's for us? The former Riot Grrrls?"

She nearly weeps when I nod.

"Finally," she says. Then she gets her story out in a burst, a last gasp of the old language.

She holds out her hands, palms up. I stand up from my lounge chair, and put my palms on hers. She expects something like a jolt, a burst of electricity between our skin, so she gasps and jerks her head back. Nothing like that has happened; that's not what happens when the thing is passed. But she expects it, so she creates it.

She pulls her hands away, wipes them on her pants. Then she opens her mouth.

"How does it feel? It feels blind."

A Bikini Kill song, "Feels Blind." Not in Lisa's voice though. The entire song, the exact notes and instruments and arrangement, all coming from her.

Lisa closes her mouth, and her body shakes in laughter. Or maybe tears.

I had both. When I opened my mouth six weeks ago and heard Sleater-Kinney's "Things You Say" issue forth, not from my own voice, no, but the recorded song from the 1997 album, I cried. For a moment, it was a cry of joy. Like I was an actual musician, able to turn emotion into sound. But then it was a cry of fright. The feeling of it, like ants crawling in my insides, wasps buzzing in my chest. They call viruses bugs, and maybe that's why. But it's not just one bug, it's a thousand, a million, a drone of wings and words we don't understand.

And the fear of the unknown, yes. That was scary. When I took to the internet to see if I was crazy, I saw local news reports and crime blotters, middle-aged women committed to hospitals and confined to drunk tanks, singing in strange, inhuman ways. They were women gone wild, mothers and wives snapping, weirdo leftists faking for attention. Just like women do.

But I saw what it could be. I recorded some tests. I posted them, signed them with "Girls to the Front." In one, I used the terms we'd build around: Sirens, sailors.

Now, I hand Lisa a room key, then gesture to the bar.

"My name is Lisa. I was seventeen when I found a Riot Grrrl group in Kansas City. It was 1991. We met in a girl's basement, where it smelled like a backed-up sump pump and fruit roll-ups. I brought my twin sister, got us out of the house, which was always the goal. Our group talked about how everyone encouraged girls to be teachers, and encouraged boys to be lawyers. We talked about how to get birth control, and what we could carry as weapons. We talked about the senior that everyone knew had raped a few freshmen girls, and how those girls didn't say a word. We went to punk shows, linked arms, pushed forward past all the moshing boys, screamed "Girls to the Front," just like Bikini Kill did. We made plans: volunteer at a women's shelter, fundraise for the food bank. That group saw me, saw the core of me and not the skin and shape. But as soon as we got started, the whole thing began collapsing. Our groups were all over the media. The things they said. The ridicule, the hysteria. We were just girls, but even our soft rebellion couldn't be borne. So the group shattered, and it was just me and my sister again.

"My sailor is a man named Tom."

Lisa and I are out on the patio the next day, under umbrellas, sipping cocktails of our making, when another one shows up.

"It's not true, is it?"

This new woman knows the answer, or she would not be here. This is the game we play, us women, pretending at seeking truth when we know it intimately, immediately. Playing at being led, when we know how to lead.

I nod, and I feel Lisa smile.

"You can pass this thing? And it can…it can make music?"

"You've got your words, but they make you stuck," says my body, my mouth, my magic.

She softens, like Lisa did, though she hardens again just as quickly. Hearing a song from a person's mouth, beyond the words and melody, the technology and tools, will turn even the most modern progressive into a medieval witch hunter, a loose queue into a pitchforked mob. A willing acolyte into a skeptic.

"Why is this happening?" She's short, the shape of a diamond, the color of sand. "And why to us?"

I shrug. The why doesn't matter. The what matters. The how. The who.

"Can it really do what you say? The whole Siren thing?"

I don't sing, or shrug, or sigh. I just look at her.

Her head hangs, brown ombré hair covering her face. She looks at her hands. Calculations are being made, and those are private, the personal costs of faith, of desire, of need. Weighed against our given rules, our laws.

I had done the same. I added up my stats: forty-seven years, two marriages, no children. A middling 401K and five feet of desk in my company's open-concept office and a West Des Moines apartment in a building filled with widows and college students. An unremarkable face of freckles and crows-feet, a torso that morphs from apple to pear shapes and back, a pair of duck feet with fallen arches. All of those things against this new fact of my biology, one that could erase the negatives, boost the positives. Hell, it could change the whole math. Blow up the equation.

The new woman, Tara, blurts out her story. And then she waits.

I don't get up this time. I just extend my hand. Strangers come to town and meet their like. She doesn't jerk back or do any of the dramatics. Just accepts what I give. When she opens her mouth, and out comes a Bratmobile song, and out pops a wide grin showing sharp teeth, we've got our third Siren.

"I'm Tara. My group was in Denver. I was only sixteen, but I'd been going to punk shows for years. Getting groped and beat up by all the guys in the mosh pits. My parents made me go to church on Sundays, dress up in a flower dress and pull my bleached hair back and listen to my uncle give the sermon. I'd watch him and think of what he'd made me do. I didn't tell anyone until I met my Riot Grrrl group. They listened. They believed me. They shared their own stories. Some girls wrote poetry and stories, and I tried writing songs. I felt like I could do anything when I was with them. Then one of the girl's parents saw an article about Riot Grrrl, the one with a chapter member topless and marker all over her body. They thought we were pornographers, lesbians, satanists. We broke up after that, and I was alone again.

"My sailor is Uncle Charlie."

By the end of the week, we have six. The most recent one, Jen, she brought a print-out of a post I did. She'd highlighted one section: "The virus is a gift. Biology is finally catching up with our desires. This is so much more than us being a human record player. This is girls to the front, in a very real way. We can be magicians without the hokum, heroes without capes. We will be Sirens."

She says she wants this, wants power. All of them do. So I give it to them. We lose the old speak, take on music as language.

If I was a man, I'd be videotaping this process. Laying my hands on each of these women and healing them with power. I'd wear bedazzled suits and snakeskin boots as I flailed about, speaking in what could only be called tongues. I'd use the videos to bilk thousands of their savings: gimme your money, gimme your love, and you'll be saved too.

Right about now I'd also start laying the groundwork for the sex stuff. Building a mythology around my healing hands, and how they must, just must be kept strong and healthy by letting them roam free over teenage tits and ass.

And don't forget the doomsday prophecies. I'd be full of them. The world would be doomed to burn in fire, by aliens or comets or nerve gas, in a period of months or years. So it'd give us a ticking clock, with plenty of time to buy our island and get our orgies in before slurping down that poison juice.

But I'm a woman. So I get to work. We get to work.

The six of us, we set up the common room in the lower level of the hotel. It's an ugly conference room and kitchen, with wood paneling and gray rubber carpet. We collect snacks and drinks, set up our laptops and a projector, start supply stations in each corner.

I remember the meeting space in the rental house on Dubuque Street in Iowa City in 1991. A group of us, college freshmen like me and a few high schoolers. Purple shag carpet under our legs and hands, mice and bats scratching behind the walls. Zines spread in front of us. Bikini Kill on the cassette deck. We took turns sharing stories. The things that happened at night in our dark bedrooms, or in fraternity houses, or backseats. The things we did to our bodies, starving and cutting and hating. The things we heard from men, from women, from those in power. The things we wanted to do different.

Now, Tara and Jen bring old zines they'd collected and kept. Black and white xeroxed copies of song lyrics, stories, screeds. My favorites had been cut-out magazine ads, showing skinny girl bodies in bikinis, dead girl bodies hawking purses, disembodied hands and asses selling cheeseburgers. All pasted next to Huggy Bear and Heavens to Betsy lyrics, screeched *fuck-you*'s to the world we were growing up in.

We pin them up to the wall. If we were still living our old lives, speaking the language of forty-something middle-class women, we'd call it our dream board, our cry to the universe, our manifestation station. We don't call it anything now. The wall of zines and memories doesn't need a name.

Each morning, I slide a written brief under each of their room doors.

"Music acts on all areas of our brains," I say through the typed copy. "It makes us physically move. It picks at our memory. It activates our opioid center, making us feel good and reducing pain. It brings us to frisson, with raised hairs and goosebumps. And when we hear music we don't like? It releases cortisol, stressing us out. There's a biological basis, then, for the idea of music as a stimulant, an incitement to action. A lure."

We test this during the days, in our rooms or on the patio. I stream Bach, Nina Simone, Glenn Miller, the surf music from "Pulp Fiction." Our heads move, our chests curve around memories, backs cover in chills. Then I have Lisa open her mouth, sing her song. The effect magnified, demonstrating in triplicate, and we curl our spines like cats and feel our limbs turn liquid.

"We used music back then to give us voice," I say through the paper. "Now music is literally your voice. And all the power that music has over a human body and brain — you have that."

I think about a friend from the Iowa City group. I'd play her my mixed tapes while we studied for our chemistry lab. I learned the language for the effect she had on my body, discovered that I could love a woman just as much or more than a man. So I'd play her more music, hoping she would understand, hoping I wouldn't have to say the words.

Shortly after that we stopped our Riot Grrrl group, knowing we had no real power, not over the minds of men in our government, not over the mechanics of our fragile bodies. I didn't know how hollow my body was, how empty it could be, the depths of the hole inside me, not until then.

The six of us, we type on our phones if we need to communicate in words. Otherwise, we're silent. Saving our music.

"I'm Jen. I used to be Jenny, before Riot Grrrl. But then I'd play a tape I copied. The way Kathleen Hanna screamed over the guitars and drums, it had me jumping, kicking, pounding my pillow. I'd feel the veins threaten my throat and forehead, the bones in my spine expand. I wasn't a Jenny anymore. For the seconds of a song I felt real. And it made me seek out others, you know? I found a group in Lansing. There were hundreds popping up then around the country, all of us finding one another at shows and in the back of zines. There was no guidebook for making a Riot Grrrl group. No rules, no template. Just a dozen of us, talking, planning. We wrote letters to the editors of the city paper and the college paper. We made ads for the Rape Crisis line and the Planned Parenthood and taped them on phone poles. We bought second-hand guitars and tried to play the songs we loved. We wrote the names of rapists on bathroom walls. We wrote on our bodies, on campus bulletin boards, on sidewalks. We did all the things we could think to do. But we were still kids. Girls. And no one wanted to hear from us.

"My sailor is named Craig."

By the tenth day, we have ten women.

Everyone has picked one man, someone deserving, someone they have dreamed about, someone that's haunted them. We draw straws one night in the common room after eating takeout pizza and drinking red wine. And who wins the draw but Lisa, the first of us.

"Remember learning about the Sirens?" I say in our morning briefs. "They were creatures that looked like beautiful women, and they sang to passing sailors. Any who heard them sing would throw themselves overboard, desperate to join them. What happened then? Stories differ. Some think the sailors drowned in the waters. Some think they starved to death, wanting only the Siren's music for nourishment. Some think they were eaten alive, and the Sirens' rocky island homes were littered with bones and rotting flesh. Some think they were just haunted forever."

Lisa will prepare her own brief, the story about her sailor. As much as she wants, as little as she wants. She'll share with us, so we can believe in her.

"What's missing from the Sirens' stories is the connection," I say. "Sirens sang to all sailors passing by. It didn't matter who. And in that they were monsters. A better, more powerful story would be personal. A better, more modern story would be mysterious, coded. A better story would be branded."

We research Lisa's sailor, Tom. Some of us follow him and learn his schedule. Some dig into his online life. Some get tools. I finalize our location.

And one week later, at dusk, we're ready.

Lisa uses one of our new disposable phones, dials the number we've found, and hits speaker. We stand around the phone, and we have a musk to us, the ammonia of anticipation and anger. We hear two rings, and then a male voice. Lisa opens her mouth and out comes her song.

"How does it feel? It feels blind. How does it feel, well, it feels fucking blind."

She hangs up. She's breathing hard, licking her thin lips, adrenaline a hot cloud of sweat and sweet around her. She tucks her fawn hair behind her long ears. The others touch her shoulder, rub her back. I dip my head, nudge her forward.

Lisa texts the same number. Come to me, it says, along with the address for a foreclosed house near Adel, a dozen or so miles away from our lodge.

My hands are twitching, breath hitching on the way through my chest. How does anyone believe in themselves this much? How does anyone have the gumption and the confidence and the ego to propose a theory, convince others of that theory, guide a group through the steps needed to prove that theory? I'm testing the scientific method I learned in school.

There's no time for doubt, though, now that we've started. There's only time to grab the bags we've pre-packed, zip up our black jackets and gloves, get into a couple cars and drive onto the two-lane highway. The sun's setting, leaving streaks of orange and pink, blue-black chasing them away.

And then we're there, pulling off the asphalt and onto gravel. Driving into the growing darkness of a private road that's no longer private. After some digging, I learned the owners absconded after a couple evictions and squatting arrests. Now the house is in limbo, ownership a myth that can't be attributed to the bank or the debtors.

Past the thick copse of trees, we see the old farmhouse. There's enough light to spot the peeling paint and cracked porch stairs. Birds have invaded the house; we can hear their wings and hoots in the shadows. There's an old silo in the back, the kind I used to look at in the eighties and wonder if they held nuclear missiles.

Lisa hops out of the lead car, waves us to follow. This is her show now. That's the deal. We each get our turn.

We're quick and efficient as we set up in the empty living room, dodging piles of mouse turds, epic cobwebs, and a dead squirrel. Once done, I find a place to stand against the ashy fireplace, with a clear line of sight through the cracked front window and into the main entry. The others scatter around the room, forming a sort of circle. Lisa is eerily still; I imagine she's rechecking and recalibrating those calculations in this last moment.

Lights, bouncing down the gravel. An SUV slows and stops. A figure steps out. Tom. He's in a poorly-cut suit, his padded shoulders too wide and his inseam too short. He turns in an agitated circle, his mostly-bald head moving strangely on his neck. Like a machine, a mechanical puppet, his circuitry offline.

Lisa steps onto the porch. The man stops his erratic spinning. She opens her mouth.

"As a woman I was taught to always be hungry"

I see it this time, the thrall that washes over her sailor with the Bikini Kill song. His jaw relaxes and falls open. His milky cheeks go slack. His inset eyes blink heavy. He lumbers on dead, dumb feet up the path and to the porch. He's a pile of meat cobbled together into a man's shape, animated by Lisa's song alone.

"Yeah women are well acquainted with thirst"

He follows her, onto the folding chair we've set in the center. The others set to him, tie his arms and legs with the rolls of duct tape from our bags. The song pours from Lisa's mouth, and just like I said, we see her song ripple across his skin, paths of goosebumps and raised hairs. He's drooling a bit, like any junkie that's hit the spot.

"I could eat just about anything"

Lisa unsheathes her knife.

"We might even eat your hate up like love"

It must be gratifying to see him like this, nearly incapacitated, but also horrifyingly familiar. This man was so drunk when he ran his car off the road twenty years ago the doctors had to pump his stomach. But that was the only thing they had to do to him. The passenger, though, Lisa's twin, the girl too scared to stand up to her moody brute of a boyfriend, too timid to call a cab or take his keys, too in love to see him as he was, she had her chest cracked open. The doctors held her heart in their hands before declaring it dead.

He waits in his chair, and Lisa leans over him, slowly, lovingly, full of eye contact. A few of us hold his arms, but he doesn't struggle. Doesn't fight. He seems to desire whatever Lisa wants.

The first cut sounds like scissors on paper. Lisa carves a circle, slicing through skin like red summer berries, a black-red line forming across his forehead, along his hairline, under his lip, and back up. Blood runs over his eyelids and eyelashes, but he doesn't blink. The circle done, she draws a diagonal line from one side to another, cutting through an eyebrow, the ridge of his nose, a fleshy cheek. Then, another line, from the other side.

His face is an oozing mess of an X. Lisa steps back to appraise her work. We snap our approval.

"I eat your hate like love I eat your hate like love"

The face done, Lisa pulls the rose and hedge trimmer from another bag.

Snip, and an index finger falls.

Snip, and the other hand's thumb drops.

"I eat your hate like love I eat your hate like love"

Lisa throws her head back and laughs.

I clap my hands, and when I have her attention, hold up three fingers. Three steps. No time to gloat yet.

Lisa stretches her arms in front of her chest, above her shoulders. From the last bag, she pulls out the men's athletic sock filled with a hard bar of soap. Then, singing her song, she swings.

*

Over the next few days, we watch the local newscasts and online feeds. There's a chance he won't go public. Men fear the laughter of others most, of course.

But Tom's bruised pride is outweighed by the gore, the confusion, the rage at being bested. Soon we see the headlines we seek.

Local man wounded in bizarre ritual

"They were everywhere," says survivor of strange attack

Marked man tells of brutal attack by gang of crazed women

His memory is fuzzy, so the details are too. He can't find his phone (because Lisa took it). He doesn't know why he woke in his SUV's backseat in a Denny's parking lot in Ames (where

Lisa left him). He thinks there was a group of women, dressed in black, and someone playing music or singing. But he can't remember how many women, their faces, what they did. The only thing he's sure of is the physical marks left behind. A face cut with a giant X, to mark him. Two missing digits, to slow him. A shattered pelvis, to neuter him.

But lack of confirmed detail: that doesn't stop enterprising reporters working free of oversight, seeking eyeballs and likes. This is far too salacious to skip. So the stories start, and spread.

Meanwhile, we meet in our common room, pass around beers and cupcakes and mimosas. I open my mouth for the first time in a while, and "Things You Say" is still there.

"*It is brave to feel, it is brave to be alive*"

We dance. Oh, how we dance.

"*My name is Marin. That was you guys on the news, right? Good.*

"*I was a high school senior in Albuquerque when I found Riot Grrrl. I was fat; I've always been fat. My mother put me on a diet at age seven, and my dad would point out my rolls to 'motivate' me. Fat was a death sentence, an automatic ugly, a fact that made me unlovable. But the girls in my group, they talked about the diet industry, how it was designed to make us feel worthless, how it had invaded every part of our culture and brains. Some of them had been vomiting their insides out to stay skinny. We went to grocery stores and put stickers in the fashion magazines that said: 'How can you achieve your dreams if you spend all your energy on dieting?' We'd put stickers on fitting room mirrors: 'Doesn't fit? That's the designers' fault, not yours.' I would look at myself in the mirror and touch my belly, the fat I used to want to cut off, and feel how soft and strong I was. One day we went through a J.C. Penney and knocked all the tiny, prepubescent female mannequins over. They actually had us detained and were going to arrest us. That was the end of our group.*

"Without them, I took love where I could find it.
"My sailor's name is Matt, the husband I ran from."

More strangers come to town, seeking me, seeking us. They've seen the story, asked around, did the digging that shows they need this.

Each week, we draw another name, selecting a Siren.

There's Marin, who chooses Matt as her sailor. When they were married, he slapped her, kicked her, pushed her down the stairs. She lost at least one baby that way. She had to change her name to get free. In the farmhouse, she cuts the X into his face a tiny millimeter at a time. Violence as love, just as he always said. Blood as devotion. When she pummels his pelvis, she cries.

There's Jen, who chooses Craig. She saw him routinely at her morning coffee stop. When she started seeing him in her neighborhood, walking the sidewalks and lingering, she assumed he'd moved nearby. When she found remnants of him in her house, dead flowers spelling out her name, underwear sliced to pieces, a dildo in her bathtub, she reported him, but what could they do? When she brought a date home, and woke to see her tires slashed and naked pictures in her mailbox, she retreated inward, far inside, trapped. At the farmhouse, she cuts little lines, a dotted circle with a dotted X. She rubs his blood on his lips, the only kiss she'll ever give him.

There's Tara too, and her uncle Charlie. She was a buxom thirteen-year-old, and he held her breasts in his palm, said they weren't the breasts of a teenager but a woman, one ready to be treated like a woman. In the farmhouse, she cuts down to the bone. She slips his severed fingers into her pockets, and I'll see her hands in her pockets in the coming weeks.

Every new sailor gets more press. Every week, more Sirens join us.

And I'm happy. This is what happiness feels like, this feeling of a hole filled. It's the feeling of a prophecy fulfilled, too; back in the nineties, they called us radicals, feminazis, lesbian witches, man-hating whores. Because we were young girls talking instead of hair-pulling, moshing instead of smiling. Yeah, it fell apart then. But now look at us. Just look at us.

"You guys are the vigilantes, right? Or Sirens, sure. Whatever you want to call it. You'll help me?

"I'm Amelia. I was a teenager fucking around, and had an abortion. Around the same time I realized I was a lesbian. I was kicked out of my house outside Seattle for both reasons. Riot Grrrl took me in. When we broke up, it was ok. I'd become tougher, and I stayed in touch with everyone. But it's like the whole world has forgotten about us. It's not fair.

"Jackson. He's my sailor. When can I hurt him?"

When it starts to go to shit, I don't admit it at first.

We're at the farmhouse, and Amelia is slicing up Jackson good. He spotted her at an abortion clinic a year ago, shepherding her teenage neighbor through the protesters. He's been trolling her online ever since. She's had death threats, bomb threats, rape threats. He's published her address, her social security number, her banks and loans and gym membership. Her credit is increasingly a wreck. She's been afraid to leave her house, afraid to stay.

Now she's come alive, drawing a near-perfect circle in his skin.

We're consistent, in our research, and our strength. So we may have become complacent. Our Siren thrall has kept the men docile and doting throughout the surgeries. We don't see the need to hold Jackson down, trusting the duct tape and Amelia's song from Huggy Bear to keep him restrained.

But as Amelia finishes her cuts and lines up his fat thumb between the blades, a shudder goes through him. He seems to wake as from a long summer's nap, and he wakes into a scream.

We're stunned. Consistency bred complacency. But also sloppy security. We're not covering our faces or even our hair. Why bother, right, when our power is absolute?

We've been thinking like men, cocky with correlation, not causation.

Jackson has time to scan the room with his thick glasses and distended pupils, to see all of us, the group of a few dozen middle-aged women who are frozen in inaction. His skinny limbs fight against the tape, and it won't be long until it rips.

Jen and Marin open their mouths to sing, try to get him back under, but nothing comes out, no music, so he doesn't calm or slump, he screams louder, straining at the tape, rocking back and forth on the chair, and Amelia hushes the others and tries singing on her own, but it's not working, why isn't it working, why, and they're looking at me, and oh fuck, now what, and they're gesturing, hurry up, figure this out, why isn't he calm, he sees us, and before I can gain control, right as I figure out what I'll do, I'll take an empty bag, throw it over his head, block his vision, so at least we can cut the chances of him identifying us, before I crouch down to grab one of the black duffels, there's a crack, and the screaming stops, and Jackson tilts, falls, clatters to the floor in a crunch of flesh and metal.

In the quiet after, I hear locusts outside, the buzz of their song.

We stare at Jackson, and the red seeping from his head.

The Sirens, they're covering their mouths, they're looking at me, they're freaking out. Except for Amelia, who's holding something in her hands and breathing hard. It looks like a rock, or a thick section of tree branch, something that was pushed to the edges of the room when we swept the initial debris. Amelia only has eyes for her sailor.

And now, we have a dead man on our hands.

*

The next morning I sit on the patio, watching the water. Lisa, Jen, and Tara join me. Amelia is there too. She has a punched-in look to her, flattened and bruised. I see her typing on her phone, and she shows me: I killed him. I killed him. I killed him.

The old speak is so limited. Reading that, I can't tell if she's guilty, or gloating. Her face contorts in foreign ways. I see her last night, on the shore of Lake Red Rock, hacking away at Jackson with our trimmer and a saw we scrounged up, so the corpse will look nothing like our other sailors. So no one can tie them together.

I promised the women, said this power could give them personal, but still anonymous, vengeance. We'd lure the men, mark them, and never be known. No one would ever suspect middle-aged women of such violence, such bravery.

On the deck, we're all afraid to open our mouths. Is the music still there? Is our Riot Grrrl revival as dead as our first go?

No. Not possible. That's what we think as we sit quietly in the sun, our mouths closed tight.

*

Over the next days, a few things happen.

We stop drawing sailor names. We stop getting new women showing up. A couple of our number disappear in the night, spooked. The rest of us dump our old phones, our laptops. We grind to a halt.

And in that void, reporters, our friends in spreading the message, are now threatening our anonymity. A teenager has reported seeing two women leave an old Taurus in a Bakers' Square parking lot one night. The teenager, he's curious, so he goes to look at the Taurus. And would you look at that, there's a passed out, bleeding Uncle Charlie in the back. The teenager, he's confident he can give the police a sketch of the two women. They weren't wearing hoods or nothing.

At the same time, some of the Sirens get texts and messages, from friends, family, acquaintances. Police are digging for grudges against the victims, skeletons in closets. They're getting a few of our names.

I've opened my mouth in private, in my own room. No music comes out.

The few women who've stayed, they're waiting for me to solve this. They're probably conducting their own tests, have found what I've found. The virus seems to be gone. So now what do we do? No power, and a death on our hands?

The downside of being a cult leader, perhaps, even a feminist vigilante cult: they all expect the idiot who volunteered to lead to actually, well, lead.

In that house in Iowa City, at the impatient edge of nineteen, I had thought about hurting people. I thought about how nice it would be to punch some of the buffoons who talked over me in classes, the guys that cornered girls in The Fieldhouse and The Union bars, the professor that liked to brush his groin against female backs. Being in Riot Grrrl, doing something, even if it was just talking to other girls, that helped.

Young, I was all heart and heat and rage. We all were. Maybe that's why we couldn't sustain our groups, especially in the face of leering adults that thought us foolish and broken.

And after twenty-eight years, a boring hallucination of a life, where I push everything inside, own every injustice and let it digest me slowly, where that heat cooled and that heart slowed, that rage turned a solid and strong lining to all my organs; when I found a way to let that out, a way that others like me could release their own pressure, do things right…why wouldn't I have run with this magic viral power? Why wouldn't I let it go to my head?

I drink on that hotel patio, with the ones who are left. Marin, Tara, Lisa, Jen. Amelia too. At first we're deathly quiet, but as the days pass and the news gets worse, we start to talk. The old speak again. It brings us to tears.

I tell them: It's ok to leave.

I tell them: It's ok to go back to your lives.

I tell them: It's ok to ditch your old life too, try something new, flee.

I tell them: I'm sorry. I got it wrong. We're not Sirens. Maybe we never were.

Amelia, she shakes her head. "There's nothing to go back to, not for me."

Jen, she leaks snot mixed with tears. "It was so empty. Just a bunch of holes that I was always trying to fill."

Marin. "Nothing will feel as good as what we did."

Tara. "The feel of having terror reversed. Seeing that on his face."

Lisa. "There's no normal now, not anymore."

And as they talk, I remember the images of Sirens you always see in textbooks. Beautiful, nubile women. Mermaid-type creatures. Even pretty heads on bird bodies. Something that tricked you into letting your guard down.

But then I remember their opposite. The Furies. Ugly, winged women, with snakes for hair and eyes dripping blood. Fangs and claws. Nothing more terrible than an unattractive woman who doesn't smile, who won't pretend, who only wants vengeance.

And then I understand. We had the wrong myth the whole time.

*

Noon, a week later.

The six of us, we've cleared out our rooms, tidied up the common room. Left our keys on the front desk, and loaded up the Jeep, the only car we didn't sell.

Every cult's downfall is a home base, after all. Without a ranch to storm, or a compound to breach, we'll be more nimble, more safe.

Driving takes us out of the small lake town and across central Iowa. Outside our car windows the sky darkens, quickly, without remorse, as it does in Iowa summers. A low rumble of thunder to the east, where we head.

On the way, I tell the other women in the car about me.

I'm June Kullen. I was a Riot Grrrl at nineteen, in Iowa City. But long before that, I was a kid who walked home from elementary school, used my key to get in the house, and babysat myself until my parents got home from work. One afternoon, right as I got in the house, there was a phone call. I picked it up and heard heavy breathing. Kind of wet. At first I thought he had a cold, or sinus trouble. I should have hung up, but I kept saying hello like a dolt, thinking he had a message, something important, because he was laboring so hard to get it out. "Little girl like you," the man finally said. "Shouldn't be left alone." Then his voice got all choked, strangled, and he moaned long and hard. I held that phone as he kept breathing, fast, and then he was laughing, laughing at me, the dumb girl who kept on listening. He laughed and laughed, then hung up. I ran to my bedroom, and curled into the back of my closet. I stayed there until my mom and dad came home, then I brushed myself off, washed my face, and went down to dinner.

The house is behind an elementary school on the east side, with cheerful blue paint and yellow lilies growing along the porch. Roses too, their thorns hidden under the vibrant cherry red. The house is three down from my childhood home.

After a few months of those breathy, choked calls, I saw Mr. Levin at a block party. I recognized his voice. He kept calling, and I kept pretending I didn't know who it was, kept answering.

Mr. Levin is now seventy-three years old, retired, a father to three, a grandfather to ten. Mr. Levin, a born and bred Des Moines man, who worked in the tire plant before Firestone shut it down. Mr. Levin, a deacon at his church, an author of two self-published spy novels, a golf fanatic. Mr. Levin, the man who called me every day when I was eight, and told me what little girls should and shouldn't do.

The wind is picking up outside our Jeep, parked directly opposite Mr. Levin's house.

I call him from the car.

A rough male voice answers with a clipped hello. His voice has the type of scratch that denotes a lifelong habit, the brusqueness that shows his warm opinion of himself and his time.

I just breathe for a minute, heavy and wet, a bit of a moan behind it.

"Who the hell is this," he says.

"Old men shouldn't be left alone," I say.

There's silence on the other line, and I laugh and laugh.

"What do you want," he says, but I hang up.

One side of the sky is white-blue, and the other black-blue. The wind is gone.

Marin picks up the camera, and we all exit the car. The six of us, heading straight for his front door.

When he answers, a tall man with sagging jowls, age-spotted cheeks, a paunch, I hold out my hand to shake. His response is automatic, the glad handing of a man in the world. Only after he shakes does he really see us, see the red we've painted under our eyes, the tight coils of our hair, the black shirts with painted wings. Only then does he recoil.

But I grip tight, and push him further into the house. When he resists, the others join.

Lisa brings out the sign. Amelia brings out the string. Jen brings out the needle. Marin records everything.

Outside, a distant wail. It's the tornado siren. It blares, a whoop and a wail that dips and rises. Like music. We used to be kin, that tool and I.

But there comes a time when music isn't enough.

Mr. Levin is starting to howl now, so I sing, in my own voice, just a tiny bit.

"*Dig me out, dig me in, out of this mess, baby out of my head.*" Not nearly as beautifully as Sleater-Kinney, of course, but that's ok. The song is mine to enjoy again. Just a song.

In front of me is just a man, an old man, useless and harmless. But back then, his voice held me under his thrall. I heard from him that I was a thing to terrorize, a thing to use. I was there for his pleasure. Me, the dolls I loved and the games I played at school and the joy I found in adding up figures, they were nothing. He wasn't the last man to teach me my worth. But he was the first.

I kneel down, look at him, watch his pupils.

"Dig me out, dig me in, out of my body, out of my skin"

Outside the siren blares, and inside, the Fury does not kill a man, but shows him he is powerless.

*

We're driving now, the six of us. Hitting the road, going where we're called.

We left Mr. Levin on his front porch. His face was marked, yes. And fingers snipped. And pelvis punched again and again.

But we also left something else. The sign was tied to a string, and we sewed that string into the skin around his neck and chest. The entire length of that thing, in a beautiful cross-stitched pattern. Lisa showed me how; she used to do it on tea towels for stress relief.

On the sign, I wrote out why he had been targeted. I signed it, "Girls to the Front."

Now, we drive, and we pick who will be next, and we watch our messages. Those who want to join us, of any age, they will understand the code we've left, will know how to get in touch with us.

We are vigilantes, yes. I am someone who will turn my rage into damage. So are my Furies.

Will you?

If you, stranger, come to our traveling town, will you take this knife? Here, hold it. Feel its weight. Know that it can unclench your teeth, unblush your cheeks. Your dreams, where you cry and scream and fight, where all the anger and rage you've buried inside comes out, and you wake for a moment with such release and relief... You know those dreams? Choosing a man, from all the men in the world, from all in your life, choosing one to mark; that can make those dreams recede, make your sleep smooth and dreamless. That can help you dig out of your darkness, find your way into the sunlight.

Are you ready?

Acknowledgments

Thank you to the editors of the following publications in which these stories, often in different forms, first appeared:

Angst Zine: "Wintersong";
Barrelhouse: "Typical Girls";
Variety Pack: "Exile in Guyville."

*

Thank you to Peter Conners, Justine Alfano, Michelle Dashevsky, Kathryn Bratt-Pfotenhauer, Genevieve Hartman, and all who work at and with BOA Editions. Thank you to Sandy Knight for her beautiful cover design, and Marie Buckley for her startlingly eerie original art.

Thank you to Gwen E. Kirby and Chelsea G. Summers, whose work I admire deeply.

Thank you to the musicians who inspire me, and whose songs provided titles, lyrics, and more: Liz Phair, The Slits, Broadcast, Nina Simone, Jesca Hoop, Sleater-Kinney, and Bikini Kill.

Thank you to the women and the queer community who persist and resist, in the face of acts of annihilation.

Thank you to Margaret Atwood, whose speculative fiction showed me a path.

And thank you to my friends.

*

Gratitude for the lyrics that have inspired me and that appear in this collection. All efforts have been made to obtain permissions where appropriate for the quotation of copyrighted material.

"The Deuce," Blown Deadline Productions, Rabbit Bandini Productions, Spartan Productions. 2019.

"Thelma and Louise," Pathé Entertainment, Percy Main Productions, Star Partners III Ltd. 1991.

"Blackbird," Nina Simone. From *Nina Simone with Strings*, Colpix Records, 1966. Warner Chappell Music.

"Things You Say" and "Dig Me Out," Sleater-Kinney. From *Dig Me Out*, Kill Rock Stars, 1997. BMG.

"Feels Blind," Bikini Kill. From *Revolution Girl Style Now*, Bikini Kill Records, 1991. Babe Anderson.

About the Author

Amy Lee Lillard is the author of three books: *Exile in Guyville*, *A Grotesque Animal*, and *Dig Me Out*. Her work also appears in *Vox, LitHub, Barrelhouse, Foglifter, Epiphany, Off Assignment, Autostraddle,* and more. She received an Iowa Author Award in 2023 and was named one of Epiphany's Breakout 8 Writers in 2018.

Amy is the co-creator of Broads and Books Productions. She's worked as a copywriter and marketer for twenty-five years. And at this very moment, she's probably listening to punk music.

BOA Editions, Ltd.
American Reader Series

Colophon

BOA Editions, Ltd., a not-for-profit publisher of poetry and other literary works, fosters readership and appreciation of contemporary literature. By identifying, cultivating, and publishing both new and established poets and selecting authors of unique literary talent, BOA brings high-quality literature to the public.

Support for this effort comes from the sale of its publications, grant funding, and private donations.

~

The publication of this book is made possible, in part, by the special support of the following individuals:

Anonymous

June C. Baker

Angela Bonazinga & Catherine Lewis

Daniel R. Cawley

Joseph C. Finetti & Maria G. Mastrosimone

Margaret B. Heminway

Charles Hertrick & Joan Gerrity

Nora A. Jones

Paul LaFerriere & Dorrie Parini, *in honor of Bill Waddell*

Barbara Lovenheim

Joe McElveney

David W. Ryon

John H. Schultz

Meredith & Adam Smith

William Waddell & Linda Rubel